HER CHOSEN PROTECTOR

NIGHT STORM, BOOK THREE

CAITLYN O'LEARY

© Copyright 2020 Caitlyn O'Leary
All rights reserved.
All cover art and logo © Copyright 2020
By Passionately Kind Publishing Inc.
Cover by Lori Jackson Design
Edited by Rebecca Hodgkins
Content Edited by Trenda Lundin
Cover Photo by Wander Aguiar Photography

All rights reserved. No part of this book may be reproduced in any form or by any electronic or mechanical means, including information storage and retrieval systems—except in the case of brief quotations embodied in critical articles or reviews—without permission in writing from the author.

This book is a work of fiction. The names, characters, and places portrayed in this book are entirely products of the author's imagination or used fictitiously. Any resemblance to actual events, locales or persons, living or dead, is entirely coincidental and not intended by the author.

The unauthorized reproduction or distribution of this copyrighted work is illegal. Criminal copyright infringement, including infringement without monetary gain, is investigated by the FBI and is punishable by up to five years in federal prison and a fine of $250,000.

If you find any eBooks being sold or shared illegally, please contact the author at Caitlyn@CaitlynOLeary.com.

 Created with Vellum

To everyone out there struggling to be calm and kind in turbulent times, your acceptance and bravery shines through. You are not alone.

SYNOPSIS

Can he overcome his pain and heartbreak in time to save the woman he loves?

Life had always come easy to Navy SEAL Asher Thorne, until an overwhelming loss made him doubt his ability to protect the ones he loved. Devastated, he has no choice but to push on and do his duty.

Eden York's job as a translator took a dangerous turn when she was asked to work on a highly confidential project in Venezuela. She thought she knew the risks, but with the fate of a nation at stake, they didn't matter—she had to help.

Eden's international team of experts is targeted by terrorists, trapping her in an unimaginable situation. When Asher's team is sent in to rescue them, he wants to believe that this time will be different, this time he can protect someone worth saving, even if he has to sacrifice his own life to do it.

PROLOGUE

Asher Thorne didn't flinch at the distinctive sound of a grease gun being fired. The shots came at an even cadence as he tramped up the soggy, muddy logging trail toward his older brother's cabin. As he got closer the shots began to fire more rapidly until they were soon just one ceaseless, incessant noise.

"You're going to start a fire," he shouted as he looked over the chaos in the clearing in front of the cabin.

"It's raining." Law's voice was low, but Asher heard him even over the rain and gunfire. His baby brother had massacred eight spruce trees by Asher's count—the branches, boughs, and needles were strewn everywhere. Lawson continued to shoot at one tall tree as he leaned his hip against the porch rail of the cabin. His strength made it easy for him to spray the gun forward and back, finally felling another tree.

"Is this making you feel any better?" Ash asked.

"Maybe. I haven't decided." His words were coated with bitterness.

Asher swung his duffel off his shoulder and walked past his brother up the stairs into Xavier's cabin. It had been their brother's sanctuary. The furnishings were sparse, but when Xavier needed a chance to unwind after a mission, this is where he always ended up. Ash had never understood the appeal of the ass-end of Manitoba, Canada. It wasn't surprising that after his death he and Law had ended up here, trying to figure out what had been going on in Xave's head.

The shooting finally stopped, and the stomp of Law's boots sounded on the stairs right before the door slammed open.

"What the fuck was he thinking?" Law yelled into the small space.

Asher didn't answer. Law must have been here a while, since there was already a fire going in the woodstove. Ash checked the contents in the pan on top of the stove.

"Don't ignore me."

"You're tough to ignore," Asher said mildly as he stirred the pea soup. Law hated the stuff, but it had been Xavier's favorite. Asher really wasn't surprised that his little brother was eating the stuff. It was basic instinct to do anything to feel closer to a deceased loved one, no matter how mad you were at them. Asher found a chipped bowl and a tin mug and ladled some of the soup. He placed it on the solid pine table that Xavier had built.

"Sit down," he commanded his brother as he pushed

out a chair for him with his foot. Law fished out two spoons from a drawer and handed one to Asher then sat. They ate in silence. When his brother picked up his bowl and sucked down the last of its contents with a loud slurp, Asher felt something shift inside his chest. For just a moment, his pain lifted.

Law set down his bowl and looked up, showing a sign of life. "It used to annoy the shit out of Maman when Xavier would do that."

"Yeah, it cracked me up that even when he was well over six feet tall, she'd still whap him on the shoulder with her wooden spoon."

"It was the only thing he ever did wrong in her eyes," Law said. "He was such a suck-up."

They both smiled. It felt good. For one blessed moment, it felt *good*. Then Law took a deep breath and blew it out slowly through his nose.

"How could he let her down so badly? How could he let *us* down? He was Delta for fuck's sake!"

The bowl flew across the room before crashing against the log wall. Law was out of his seat, the chair on the floor, as he grabbed the hot pan off the stove and threw that against the opposite wall, a green spray of pea soup following in its wake.

"Why?" he bellowed. "Goddamn you, Xave. I still needed you!"

Asher felt his heart breaking. It was an actual physical pain in his chest.

Unshed tears glittered in Law's eyes as he turned to

Ash. "Why didn't he come to us? What could have been so bad that he couldn't have come to us?"

The pain in his chest tripled in size. It was the same question Asher had been asking himself since the day he'd heard about Xavier's suicide. How could he have failed his big brother so badly?

"How could he have done this to Maman?" Law cried out. He stood there, his chest heaving, his arms stretched out from his body, his hands fisted. "How is she surviving this?"

"She doesn't know," Ash whispered as he cautiously walked over to stand in front of his large brother.

"You didn't tell her that Xavier killed himself?" Law whispered.

Asher shook his head. "Since she's over in Belgium, and you were on a mission, they notified me first. I told her. I said he died during a training exercise."

Law gripped his shoulder. "Thank God you did that. I talked to her, but she was so broken up, we never discussed how he died." Law's fingers clenched tighter. "We just talked about Xavier, ya' know? Hell, half the time she was talking French so fast I couldn't understand her."

Ash had understood every word she'd said. He'd talked to her in French for hours. First, she'd lost dad, and now Xavier. He had to get her to the States.

"I don't get it, Ash. I don't understand how his life could have come to that. I just don't get why he couldn't have reached out to us. I spoke to him three days before. He kept asking about me. Wanted to know if I was all right. He picked at me to open up. I should have known to turn it around." Law's voice was thick with tears. He collapsed on the sagging piece of furniture trying to pass as a sofa, his head in his hands. Ash sat down next to him so he could hear his next whispered words. "It's a gut punch knowing I failed him."

He looked up at Asher with a tortured expression.

Asher couldn't take it a moment longer. He pulled his kid brother into his arms, trying to think of the right words. Words that would exonerate Law. Give him solace. Something that would never be possible for himself.

"Law, you know Xavier. He was strong. He would never have admitted something was wrong. Our brother never knew how to bend, so the winds just kept coming at him until that day he shattered. I don't think he ever saw it coming."

It took a moment for Ash to understand what Law was saying into his shoulder. Finally, he understood him.

"Yes, Brother, I promise to come to you if the winds ever get too strong. I promise."

CHAPTER 1

Asher had made sure to buckle into the jump seat next to Ezio when they'd boarded the plane. The man had just transferred in from the Omega Sky team, and even though there was a lot of hype surrounding him, it still remained to be seen if he could cut it on their Night Storm SEAL team.

Leo Perez was on Asher's other side. He was reading a worn paperback by Steinbeck. The man would read and re-read a book until the pages fell out during each stint abroad. This time it was *Cannery Row*, the last mission it had been *The Great Santini* by Pat Conroy. Asher thought that maybe he should read something; it sure would be better than having all the "what ifs" swirl through his head.

"What do you think of that, Ash?" Cullen Lyons called out from the jump seat directly across from him.

It took a beat for him to respond. Luckily, it was Cullen, so he knew what he needed to say. "Sounds like a pile of lies to me," Asher replied. He had no idea what Cullen had said, but that answer was usually a safe bet.

Raiden Sato raised his eyebrow, "There you have it, Nic. Thorne agrees with me—there's no way that Cullen took the first place trophy in a karaoke contest in the middle of a swamp."

"I said it was a wet t-shirt karaoke contest. Get the story straight, Raiden." Cullen griped. "Over two-thirds of the audience were women and they liked what they saw." Cullen flexed his biceps. "That, along with my superb singing voice, guaranteed me a win."

"I'm with Asher; there's no such thing as a wet t-shirt karaoke contest," Kane McNamara said, never looking up from his computer tablet.

"Florida," Cullen said to Kane. "You need to go down to the bars in Florida. They have everything. I had an option to sing with an alligator on a leash. I would have, except the girl who had just gone before me had dibs on him. She decided to take him home. Apparently, her mama and auntie had an alligator breeding program going on at their place and that bull would make fine babies."

Everybody felt the landing gear lower, which stopped the conversation. That was fine by Asher. He was absolutely goddamn sure that Cullen would soon be telling them that there had been sparklers shooting out of his ass during his karaoke performance.

All things considered though? Asher had heard Cullen's singing voice—chances were that he'd won plenty of karaoke contests. *But seriously, an alligator?*

Asher looked down at the luminous dial of his watch. Oh-one-hundred hours, and they were supposed to meet their transport at oh-four-hundred on the outskirts of Caracas, Venezuela. Kane's face was illuminated by his tablet; for once he looked satisfied by what he was seeing. That was a nice change. Maybe that meant they'd get more info when they touched down in the middle of El Avila National Park.

Hopefully, things were looking up for the group of humanitarians they were going into rescue. When Asher had first heard about the group, he'd been dubious about their motives. Bankers and accountants going into Venezuela to halt the mass exodus of people from the country and maybe, possibly, help them get back on track? Yeah, sure, next he'd hear about purple pigs flying.

But these people from the International Money Fund and the World Bank were the real deal. They had financial aid workers dedicated to lifting up the forgotten and suffering people around the world. These humanitarian money-types were the people that Ash and his team were going to save.

"Does he ever quit talking?" Ezio Stark asked quietly as he tilted his head toward Cullen.

Asher choked back a laugh as he looked at the new guy's subtle grin. "When the mission calls for it, he can zip it. Unfortunately, Nic Hale kept switching Cullen's channels and then lost the remote. Now, nobody can find the off button."

Cullen looked over at the two of them, then scratched his nose with his middle finger. This time, Asher laughed out loud and so did Ezio. Asher looked to his left and saw Leo put his book away. He was practically vibrating with energy. The man was always jazzed for a mission.

The plane touched down smooth as glass. The pilot on this assignment was damn good. Setting this tube down like a hummingbird on some drug runner's dirt runway in the middle of a jungle was slick.

Ash heard a click as Leo unbuckled his belt. Yep, the mission was starting. Asher reached for his belt.

Screeeeech....

The grating sound of bending metal sliced through his eardrums as the explosion sounded.

Leo pitched forward, landing hard in the center of the floor, before sliding and hitting Raiden's legs on the other side of the transport plane. Both men grunted.

"What the fuck?" Cullen yelled.

"Shit!"

"Goddammit," Kane sounded pissed. Something must have happened to Kane's computer.

"RPG?" Ezio gave a good guess.

"Landmine." Lieutenant Max Hogan's voice cut through the pandemonium.

Asher knew that the fuel wasn't stored over the wheels so they should be safe. He watched as Raiden jerked out of his straps and held onto Leo while Nic Hale held onto Raiden. Hopefully, Leo would be all right until the airplane came to a stop.

The big bird continued to skid forward on its nose, and Ash prayed they wouldn't hit another landmine because this time it would hit right under the cockpit.

His prayers weren't answered.

A second violent explosion burst out from the front of the plane, the fiery percussion hurtling through to the back.

Asher's head slammed against the metal wall behind him as the plane tipped onto its wing. He must have blacked out, because the next thing he knew, he smelled smoke, and Kane was unbuckling his belt and yanking him up into a standing position.

"You with me, Thorne?" he yelled into his face.

"Am now," he slurred. He needed to get it together. *Now!*

Ash looked around and spotted a backpack. Didn't matter if it was his or not, he grabbed it and staggered after Kane towards the breeze of the exit. Smoke roiled around him. He saw flames licking up from underneath the door of the cockpit.

"Pilots?" He croaked out the question, as he crouched and jumped to the dirt of the runway. He grunted in pain. God, that hurt. He looked around to do a headcount.

"Where's Max and Cullen? Are they going after the pilots?"

"They're going to give it a shot." Kane thrust his computer tablet at Raiden and grabbed Asher's arm. Kane forced him at least fifty meters away from the plane to where Leo was propped up under a tree.

"I'm fine," Asher heard Leo bitching. Nic had his hand pushing down on Leo's shoulder.

"You're not fine until Kane says you are," the young SEAL ground out impatiently.

"Well, I'd be better if you wouldn't press on the shoulder that Ezio just jammed back into place." Leo's sarcasm was clear.

"Fuck, Man. I'm sorry." Nic immediately pulled his hands away from Leo's body.

Leo gave a hoarse laugh like he'd pulled a big joke. Well, he couldn't be *too* wounded.

"I'd say that's one patient you don't have to worry about." Asher gave Kane a rough grin, trying to ignore the pain in his head.

"I'll have to console myself with you. You don't look so hot." Kane was clearly troubled.

"It's not me I'm worried about," he said as he looked over Kane's shoulder at the flames.

Kane turned his head too, and they both saw two figures running away from the plane.

"It's going to blow. Clear out. Now!" Max roared. He and Cullen were running full tilt toward them.

"Get back," Max yelled at them as he pointed behind them toward the forest. "Further back."

Once again, Kane grabbed at Asher.

"Help Leo," Asher ordered as he shrugged off Kane's hand. He would have helped Leo himself, but he wasn't in any shape to. He staggered toward a thick tree that was two meters in front of him and hunkered down behind it. He waited there for what seemed like hours—or was it just a millisecond?

A massive explosion reverberated throughout the

forest, followed by dead silence when it finally stopped. Not even an insect buzzed. Asher counted under his breath.

"One."

"Two."

"Three."

"Four."

A cacophony of bird-song burst through the air. They sounded angry at the man-made interruption of their sleep. Above it all, Asher heard the cry of disgruntled monkeys. Then he heard the crackle of the fire. His shoulders slumped as he closed his eyes and said a prayer in French that he'd learned at his mother's knee. He'd been praying to the Holy Mother a lot in the last six months. Now she had two more good men to watch over. He gritted his teeth as the pain tried to suck him down. Because Asher knew. He fucking *knew*, the blood of one of the good men up in heaven was on his hands.

"Hold them close *Sainte Mere de Dieu*," he quietly begged.

"Asher Thorne, you hearing me?" He lifted his head at Kane's words.

"What?"

He shook his head trying to clear it and Xavier's face floated away, just like his life's blood had.

"Ash, I was just starting to tell the lieutenant that you and Perez were injured," Kane explained.

"I'm fine," Asher said as he forced himself to stand. "It's just a bump on the head. It might or might not be a concussion, but I'll let you know if I get nauseous or start seeing double. I'm good to hike into Caracas." He kept his tone upbeat and turned his grimace into a smile.

"And if I wanted to hear from you, I would have asked you," Max glowered. He turned back to look at Kane.

"You heard Thorne," Kane said to Max, "it's just a goose egg until he pukes and passes out, that's when we worry. Meanwhile, Perez's shoulder was dislocated, but Ezio popped it back in. He's hurting, but he'll live. We've already started divvying up his backpack contents to give his shoulder a rest."

Max looked at Asher dubiously, but he nodded.

Ash looked around the small clearing, taking in the expressions on everyone's faces. They were all either blank or somber. This was not how the mission was supposed to have started.

"Anything else?"

"I'm going to stick with Asher, and Raiden's got Leo. We'll be able to assist them if they have any issues making it to the rendezvous point."

Max nodded again. "We'll need to move fast. We've definitely made an entrance. Venezuelan authorities are going to be out after us."

"The FAES, right? The president's secret police?" Nic asked.

"That's my take. They're going to shoot first and never bother asking questions," Max sighed.

"Lovely," Cullen said sarcastically. "They're nothing but street thugs with badges. This whole set-up in

Caracas stinks." He hiked up his rifle, so it sat flush against his body, eager to take retribution.

Another explosion sounded. Flames shot higher.

Every team member took a moment to look backwards to where the night sky burst brightly in an angry inferno. Asher saw his commander's jaw clench. As their leader, Ash knew that Max took the loss of men on a mission as a personal failure, but every man on the Night Storm team felt the loss just as deeply. They might've only met the pilot and co-pilot tonight, but still for a few hours, they'd been members of their team, and they had died.

It hurt.

He could swear he heard Xavier grunting in agreement.

God, how bad had he hit his head?

After an hour of sucking down vomit, Asher heard blessed words from Max.

"Hold up. I want to have Kane give us an updated intel briefing."

"Good, I think Asher needs to puke and suck down a mint, and Leo looks like he's limping, so we can take care of that while we're at it," Raiden said wryly. That was Raiden—the king of understatement. Asher flipped him the bird. However, when Raiden handed him a tin of wintergreen Altoids, he decided that the man was back on his Christmas card list.

"Thorne and Perez, sit down before you fall down, that's an order." Max rumbled. "Kane, your computer tablet still intact?"

"Yep. Take a two-minute breather and I'll have the latest info."

Raiden, who had just finished up his advanced medic training, came over to Asher to check out the bump on his head. Ash made sure not to flinch when he probed it.

"See, I told you guys it was nothing."

"Yeah, sure. It's just an itty, bitty mosquito bite," Raiden said sardonically. "For God's sake, it looks like you're going to hatch an egg." He pulled an instant cold compress out of his rucksack and squeezed it, then handed it to Asher. "Hold that against your bug bite during the briefing."

"Seems to me that you should be giving the compress to our friend Perez. He's the one that stuffed a sock down his pants," Asher smirked.

"Huh?" Raiden looked over his shoulder. "Dammit! How'd I miss that?"

"You were too busy playing nursemaid to me, and that dumbass was trying to hide his cantaloupe. Do you have another cold compress? Because if you don't, I think Leo needs mine."

"Perez!" Raiden might have whispered his shout, but it was definitely fueled with the fury of a pissed-off medic. It was clear Raiden was trying not to call Kane and Max's attention to the matter.

Nic's head swung sharply to take in Raiden's face.

Leo took a little longer to turn around. He knew what the problem was. He was busted.

Raiden stalked over to where Leo was sitting on a log with his injured leg stretched out in front of him. Asher ambled over a little more slowly. He didn't want to admit it, but his head really hurt.

Leo held up his hands. "In my defense, I didn't know how bad it was until I sat down."

Asher snorted. "That just makes you stupid."

Raiden glared at his patient as he pulled out his med kit. "Nic, go get—"

It wasn't a great surprise to anyone but Nic when Max dropped Kane's backpack next to Raiden. "Kane said to grab what you need out of his kit."

Raiden's expression didn't change as he began rifling through Kane's rucksack. "Asher, cut his pants from the bottom to his knee, let's see what we have."

"I think he's trying to give birth." Asher cut a slit in Leo's pants, then moved out of the way so Raiden could inspect the damage.

"Well, it isn't a big bruise, so that's something," he said as he gently prodded Leo's knee. "I'd say it's a burst bursa. How painful?" he asked as he examined Leo's face.

"Nothing I can't handle," Leo said confidently.

"You're so full of shit," Raiden said as he twisted the cold pack to activate it. He handed that and the stretch bandaging to Asher. "Apply it."

"Serves you right for taking your belt off early," Asher said as he carefully bandaged up his friend.

"It does," Leo agreed. His voice was tight.

Raiden leaned down, holding water and some pills. "Drink all the water with the pills," he commanded.

"Only the anti-inflammatories," Leo said.

"You'll take the ones for pain, too."

"Don't need it," Leo protested.

"You'll slow us down if you don't take it," Asher said. "We'll watch over you and make sure you don't trip on your third ball."

"I don't—"

Asher pushed his index finger into Leo's inflamed knee. Leo hissed.

"Jesus, God! Fine. Fine. I'll take the pills. I'll take the help."

"Are we going to have to set up a hospital ward here in the jungle?" Cullen asked as he walked over.

"Not for me," Asher said wryly.

"Put that compress back on your head," Raiden ordered. Asher grimaced and did so. He watched as the rest of the team gathered around. Kane sat down on the log next to Leo, giving his knee a surreptitious glance.

It always amazed Asher how Raiden didn't roll his eyes at Kane's tendency to double-check everything. As if he could read his mind, Raiden looked up at Asher and sighed. "He can't help it, he's just wired that way. God help A.J. when they have kids, she's going to have to slap him upside the head a couple of times."

"Nah, she loves me too much," Kane said confidently.

Everybody laughed. It felt good.

Too bad it couldn't last.

CHAPTER 2

"Things have changed in Caracas, and not for the better," Kane started the briefing. "The security force that was hired to babysit the coalition failed to get the group to the empty American embassy as planned."

"Why not? I thought they were just transporting them from the Venezuelan Central Bank?" Ezio frowned. "That was only ten kilometers at most. Who stopped them? Do they know if it was Maduro?"

Somebody has been doing their homework.

Max cleared his throat. Ezio rubbed the back of his neck. "Sorry, McNamara," he said to Kane. "Not my place. If I have any questions after you're done with the briefing, I'll ask."

Somebody also *knows when they're out of line.* Asher liked it. This was Ezio's first mission with Night Storm. He was normally second-in-command on his own team, so he was used to questioning everything. But it was nice he knew when to take a backseat. It was nice to know that there was good sense under those pretty-boy good looks.

Kane began again. "Nobody knows. Not US Intelligence or any of our alliance intelligence agencies. It's a crapshoot if it's Venezuelan-backed Special Action Forces or those fuckers out of Columbia that waylaid the group."

"That security team totally fucked up when they went to the American Embassy a day early to get it ready for the coalition's arrival," Kane continued. "Hell, nobody's occupied the place for a year, and having them trying to get it habitable all of a sudden was a dead giveaway. So that definitely tipped their hand that something was going on."

"Or there could have been a mole." Raiden threw down the leaf he'd been twirling between his fingers.

"Supposedly, nobody from the Venezuelan government knew about the coalition."

"I call bullshit," Asher said.

"I raise your bullshit, with a load of buffalo turds," Cullen said disgustedly. "There isn't a fucking chance in hell that the CEO of the USForce Bank setting foot on Venezuelan soil escaped the notice of either Maduro, or for that matter President-elect Guaido. Who signed off on this operation?"

"This wasn't a government-sanctioned trip. It was a humanitarian effort from the international community," Kane reminded everybody. "This group has been working together in Geneva for the last month, trying to find a way to fix the Venezuelan economy. You know this country is in turmoil. There's been a mass exodus due to starvation, disease, and crime. It's a humanitarian crisis and both Maduro and Guaido want it to stay that way until one of them is declared the winner of the contested election so they can magically *fix* things and take credit for it. Then they'll declare themselves a national hero."

"That might not be true," Asher disagreed. "The way I'm hearing it, Guaido is on the up-and-up."

"Kane is a cynical bastard. He always believes the worst until he's proved wrong." Max reminded everyone. "What we do know for sure is that Maduro is bleeding his country dry."

"How many Venezuelans have died because of that asshole?" Cullen asked bitterly. "It's almost government-sanctioned genocide."

After everything Cullen had seen in one of their last missions in Africa and being engaged to a woman who worked for Doctors Without Borders, the man was incredibly attuned to the atrocities that happened around the world. Despite his easy-go-lucky demeanor, he truly wanted to save the world. *Time to change the subject.*

"Who's hosting this meeting?" Asher asked.

"The Venezuelan Finance minister fled the country six months ago," Kane explained. "He hasn't been replaced. Right now, the provisional head of the Central Bank and the Chairman of Banco de la Gente are the hosts. According to the intel that finally fucking downloaded in the last two hours, these two ladies are straight arrows."

"Okay, now that we know the politics and the

players, where are they, and what is our role?" Asher smothered a grin—apparently, Ezio could only keep quiet for so long.

"Suzanne Azua is feeding information to us. She's the head of Banco de la Gente, and she's insisting it's a fortress and has security that will help them. The bank is between the Central Bank and the Embassy."

Kane let that sink in.

"Dammit, wasn't this supposed to go under the radar because they were having this meeting during Carnival?" Max glowered.

"That was the hope." Kane agreed. "The good news is, according to the intel, whoever has Central bank surrounded isn't making any overt moves. Which is interesting because the back wall has been demolished."

"Why aren't they going in right this minute?" Leo asked Kane.

"It's either they're waiting for tomorrow tonight," Kane said as he looked at his watch. "I mean tonight—that's when Carnival really takes off. Or they can't get ahold of Maduro."

"Is it tonight or tomorrow night?" Nic asked.

"Today is Friday," Raiden said for Kane. "The beginning of Carnival might start at sundown tonight, but they've been getting ready for this for a week. The party will go on until Sunday morning. Everybody will be hungover for church," Raiden chuckled.

"So, they have the cover of darkness and no witnesses now. If they're not holding out for Maduro's say-so, why not right now?" Leo persisted.

"They'd be seen for sure. Raiden's right, people are out setting up." Kane explained. "The secret police don't want to be that obvious."

"People are already setting up? At two-thirty in the morning before the event?" Nic asked incredulously.

"You've never been to Mardi Gras, have you?" Cullen asked.

Nic shook his head.

"They take this shit seriously. But is it going to turn into anti-government protests?" Cullen asked Kane.

Asher saw Leo shift, bending his leg. It looked like his mobility was improving.

Kane rubbed the back of his neck. "It did last year, Cullen. My sources aren't sure. Here's our problem. The coalition's security team was going to pick us up, but that's out. What's left of them are at the Central Bank. Suzann Azua is sending people she trusts to meet us. She swears we can depend on them."

Everyone, including Max, looked at Kane incredulously. "Civilians?" Max demanded.

"We don't have any choice," Kane said.

"Do you think they wear capes?" Cullen asked. "I can see it now, staid little banker suits, their hair in buns, but when they're called into action, they shake out their hair, rip off their skirts to show garter belts—"

"Shut up, you idiot," Raiden growled. "You're getting on my last nerve."

Asher saw that Kane was trying to cover a grin. Then he started speaking again.

"Look, even if they are banker ladies, they're all we've

got. The security team is either stuck at the Central Bank guarding the Banking Coalition, or they died at the Embassy. Carter from CIA is coordinating with Azua and a couple of others that he thinks are worth a damn in this type of situation."

"Who are they?" Max demanded to know.

"We've got three to choose from. The first two are Heinrich Becker and Leland Hines. Leland's the CEO of USForce Bank. He's kept his head and he and the translator have helped keep the others calm. Hines's been around the block a time or two, he was with the SAS thirty years ago. Doubt that kind of training ever goes away."

Everybody nodded. They had all served with the British special forces before—they were good men and women.

"And the translator, what's he like?" Ezio asked.

"Her. Eden York," Kane answered. "Azua and Hines have taken the leadership roles, but they couldn't have done it without York. She's the glue. She keeps the communication going. All I've got is the resume and application she gave to the International Money Fund three years ago. No background check. She speaks six languages, has degrees in political science and animal services. She was born and raised in Montana and went to school in Idaho."

"And the third?"

"Heinrich Becker. He has degrees and awards coming out his ass. He's been in charge of the International Money Fund for over ten years. It's amazing they've kept his involvement under the radar. Ten bucks says he takes the lead on all of this." Kane finally took a breath and sighed, knowing some smartass question was coming from Cullen, and he was not wrong.

"So, what should we expect from Super Banker Babes? Are they meeting us at the rendezvous point?" Cullen asked.

Kane nodded his head.

"Yes, you're going to see your ladies in garters and capes. Basically, there have only been two little changes to our mission. Instead of meeting with a security team, we'll be meeting with the SBB's. Then instead of taking the Banking Coalition from the embassy to the airport, we'll be taking them from the Central Bank."

Asher rubbed the back of his neck, then winced when his hand touched his bump—okay, goose-egg. There were a hell of a lot more than two little changes, and the way Kane couldn't meet anyone's glance proved it. This mission was FUBAR. If someone died when they were out in the field, then the mission was Fucked Up Beyond All Recognition, full-stop! *Let's not also forget Leo is more than likely out of commission.* Then, and he hated to admit it, he was not exactly in prime condition.

Kane sighed now as he looked around at the group. "One good thing is the suits have a plane on stand-by in Guyana. Once we give them notice, they can have a plane waiting in Caracas in two hours to fly them to safety."

"Exactly, Kane. We need to stay focused on the

positive. I have faith in the Super Banker Babes. They're going to come through."

Ezio looked at Cullen like he was out of his mind. Which he very possibly was.

Asher just knew there had been sparklers involved in that karaoke contest. He just knew it.

Asher must have hit his head a whole hell of a lot harder than he thought. The birds were beginning to sing, and he had just managed to slog his way through the twenty kilometers of jungle, and here he was looking at a brightly colored food truck. Ash watched as it lumbered up the last little bit of hill toward the clearing.

Even in the dim light, the garish paint job couldn't be missed. The bottom third was red, the middle of the truck was surrounded with a stripe of blue and the top third and roof were painted in yellow. Just so nobody could mistake it, the blue was covered with stars, so it was clearly a representation of the Venezuelan flag.

Asher and his team all stayed hidden.

Fuck me. A food truck? Please tell me the Super Banker Babes aren't giving us a ride in that thing.

Whoever the driver was, laid on the horn. It sounded vaguely familiar. For just a moment, Asher was back in his childhood chasing after the ice cream man with his little brother during those hot summer days. He shook his head to get back to the here and now.

"Stay put," Max whispered.

The music stopped and a woman's voice began talking in English over the loudspeaker.

"Americans, my daughter sent me. We need your help. Come out where I can see you." There was no mistaking the authority in the voice. It sounded a little like his maman's.

I definitely have a concussion.

The driver's side door opened, and a tiny woman stepped down. She wore a coral-colored pantsuit with her white hair up in a bun. Asher thought she looked like she should have been at a bridge club except for her tennis shoes. Despite the fact that she looked to be one hundred and twelve years old, she was steady on her feet.

"My daughter sent me, she is Suzanne Azua. I am her mother, Lenora. She's the president of the Banco de la Gente and she said we don't have much time to…what is the phrase?" She paused, then snapped her fingers. "Dilly-dally."

Cullen snorted with laughter.

"Cover us," Max motioned for Raiden to follow him.

"I want to go," Cullen whined. Max gave him a hard look as he and Raiden moved out into the clearing with their rifles at the ready.

She took a long look at Max and Raiden. "Is it just the two of you?"

"Ma'am, I'm Lieutenant Max Hogan, United States Navy, and this is Chief Petty Officer First Class, Raiden Sato. More of my men will be here in a few moments. Do you mind if Raiden and I have a look inside your truck?"

"It's not mine, it's my great-nephew's truck," she gave

a distracted wave. "You need to hurry." Then she pulled herself up to her full height, which was almost five feet nothing.

Asher's lip twitched. He'd bet his last dollar this was legit, but he wouldn't risk his team's lives. He continued to carefully monitor the scene in front of him through the scope of his rifle.

"She's right, they'd better hurry," Cullen whispered behind him. "I'm hungry, and I smell deep-fried empanadas and plantains."

Ash grinned. Now he recognized the smell. He really didn't think the little old lady was driving around members of Maduro's secret police in a food truck. The two SEALs coordinated their swift entrance into the front and back of the truck.

"Clear," Raiden shouted.

"Nothing," Max said clearly as he jumped out of the back of the truck.

Cullen chuckled. "She just rolled her eyes at our lieutenant."

"Señora Azua, thank you for your patience. We needed to make sure that everything was safe before we got started," Max explained.

She gave a regal nod. "Can your men come out now? We need to move quickly. My daughter and the others are surrounded at the bank by that pig of a dictator's men." Asher snorted with laughter. The lady didn't have a filter.

Max gave a nod and Asher followed the others out to where the truck was parked.

"Is this everybody?" she asked. "Just eight of you are going to save everyone?" She was clearly skeptical.

Max nodded.

"You better be good," she muttered in Spanish as she started toward the driver's door.

At the door, she turned back to the team. "We need to get to my hacienda before sunrise. People are waiting."

"Who would that be?" Max asked.

"My granddaughter and great-grandchildren." She began to open the driver's side door when Cullen stopped her.

"Maybe it would be better if I drive," Cullen suggested as he opened the truck door for her. The smartass was gone, now he was all business.

She craned her neck to look up at him. "Been driving the streets of Caracas a lot, have you?" She had a glint in her eye.

Kane coughed, trying to disguise his laugh. Everyone could see that Cullen had a fight on his hands.

"Nope, but I've driven in Brazil, Africa, and Afghanistan," Cullen answered. He was the most proficient driver on the SEAL team. Asher knew it would kill him to let this little old lady drive.

She looked him up and down. "This truck *is* unwieldy," she admitted reluctantly. Asher would bet anything she had trouble seeing over the steering wheel. "I suppose I could let you drive. Have you driven a food truck before? It took me a couple of kilometers to get used to it."

"I'm certified for all sorts of vehicles," Cullen said patiently. He was laying the charm on thick.

"Okay then. This way I can explain what I know. My daughter can do only so much. I expect you to get them to the airport. Do you understand me?"

She pointed at Max.

"Don't worry, ma'am, we're going to get all of them out of there."

Her eyes narrowed. "You'd better."

CHAPTER 3

Eden's fingers clenched longingly for the comforting feeling of her Glock 43. The woman's version of the gun fit perfectly in her hand, and she could do some real damage with it about now. She did her best to block out Schlessinger's whining and focus on what Suzanne Azua was saying to the security team member who was fishtailing the SUV around the winding streets of Caracas. Seriously, did they not know how to produce a straight road in this country?

As the black Escalade took another punishing turn, Eden York gripped the seat in front of her and struggled to listen to the Venezuelan bank president. It sounded like she was saying that somebody had been killed. At this rate, it would be all of *them* in a heap of twisted metal on the city boulevard. Was Carlson trying out for a spot on the NASCAR team?

"What? What? What?" The Swiss Finance minister yelled at her in French. *Lord save me from self-important assholes.* "Why are they trying to murder us?" the man demanded as he jabbed his fat finger in her direction. "I command that you tell me, Eden." She turned her face before spittle hit her.

I'm not going to hit him.

"Monsieur Schlessinger, I need you to stay calm so I can listen to what they're saying," she soothed.

Señora Azua was now talking on the radio that connected the three-vehicle caravan while the driver poured on the speed. He had to, because Eden saw a blue truck pull up beside them with its windows rolled down. There were at least two guns pointed at them. She braced.

Bullets sprayed along the driver's side of their Escalade, but nothing penetrated their vehicle's specially designed armor.

"They're shooting at us!" Schlessinger screamed.

"Calm down, you fool." Leland Hines barked in English from the back row of the vehicle. Eden tried to pull Schlessinger away from the window, but his meaty body was not moving away.

Eden decided to take the forceful approach. "Duck down, Maurice," Eden ordered in French.

Another round of bullets hit their vehicle.

"Hold on," the driver yelled out English.

Eden repeated the driver's command in French and Spanish for the others, since translating was what they were paying her for.

The SUV swerved right and sideswiped the front of the blue truck, causing it to careen into oncoming traffic.

Eden watched as car after car after car plowed into the truck and one another. She prayed only the bad guys were hurt. And hurt pretty damn bad.

The assholes.

"Are you still with me?" Suzanne Azua asked into the radio. "We all have to get off the highway."

People started speaking over one another on the radio, but the bank president cut through the chatter like a flaming sword through sun-warmed butter. "I heard someone say something about some of the security team being dead. I only want that person to talk."

"This is Corey Bradshaw with Nomad Security, ma'am. We finally have a count of casualties at the US Embassy. It isn't good."

"Where are you?" Suzanne demanded to know.

"Aruba."

Eden could easily see the steam coming out of Señora Azua's ears. Probably because she was just as pissed as Eden was. *Really, the head of our security high-tailed it to Aruba at the first sign of trouble and left us to be killed?*

Eden forced herself to keep listening to what he was saying. "Our people were butchered by the president's secret police. They killed everybody but one man who dragged himself into the Embassy's safe room. He's still in there. From the monitors, he was able to see what happened to his team and report back to us."

"We need an alternate plan," one of the Nomad security drivers yelled over the radio. Eden couldn't figure out who was talking.

"Your bank, Suzanne?" It was Heinrich Becker, the

chairman of the International Money Fund, the man running the show.

"That would work," Señora Azua agreed.

"What the fuck are you all talking about?" Carlson demanded to know.

"Your useless boss who ran away to Aruba says the Embassy is no longer viable," Eden shouted over the seat.

"That's right," Señora Azua bit out. "Carlson, we need to focus on getting everybody to Banco de la Gente. Bradshaw, are you aware that someone just tried to run us off the road?"

"Dammit! I need to look into this. Maybe there's someone else I can deploy." Eden heard Bradshaw's tension, and she didn't like it. He had no one—that's probably why he flew the coop. He wasn't even pretending to care what his boss was saying anymore.

Yep, we're screwed. I'm not going to scream.

Eden wanted a gun. *The only person you can ever rely on is yourself. Or family.* That was it. And she sure as hell didn't see her dad, brothers, or sisters around here right now, so she wanted her damn gun.

One-handed, Suzanne Azua grabbed for something on the floor in front of her and brought up her extremely large handbag. She shoved it over the seat to Eden.

"Find my cell phone, it's in there somewhere," she said in rapid Spanish.

Eden dug. When she found the Señora's phone, she thrust it over the seat to her, then Suzanne did a trade and stretched the radio's cord over the backseat and handed it to Eden. "See if Bradshaw comes up with something."

The bank president keyed a number into her phone and was soon giving orders to someone.

"Hector, you told me that one of our guards is a sniper. Have him get a rifle from our armory. I want him up on our roof, now! Anyone else who was ever in the military, get them up there too with a rifle. As for the rest, I need any and all guards we have at the main entrance to the bank. I want their guns drawn."

Shit, they have an armory? At a bank?

Señora Azua paused. "Dammit, do you think I don't know it's Carnival? I don't care how few guards are working, you get the rest of them to the lobby, right now." Eden thought she was going to laugh. She'd never noticed the resemblance until right now, but this kick-ass woman was just like her mother! "Hector, we'll be pulling up with three black Escalades. I want the doors open and ready for us to enter. As soon as we're all in, slam those doors shut behind us."

There was one more pause. "Good. I'm counting on you."

"Team, we have a plan," Eden said into the radio.

Through the radio, Eden could hear shots being fired.

"Who's being shot at?" she demanded.

"This is car three. I'm fine. What's the plan?" The driver's voice was hoarse. Eden recognized him as Patel.

"This is Rivers in car two, one of our tires has been blown. We can't keep this up. Tell me that we're going to be able to stop soon."

"Tell me what is going on," Schlessinger yelled at Eden in French. "Where is our security team?"

Sunbathing in Aruba.

They rounded another corner and their driver laid on the horn. Señora Azua was giving further directions to the bank.

"Eden! I demand that you answer me," Schlessinger commanded.

Eden felt her fist clench as she quelled the urge to hit the Swiss man's doughy face. *Not. Going. To. Hit. Him.* "You need to be quiet so I can hear what's going on. Our lives depend on us being calm," she enunciated every French word slowly and precisely.

"Shut your damned mouth, Maurice," the British banker barked from the back seat.

Schlessinger might not've understood English, but he caught Leland's tone. The Swiss man squeezed his lips shut, which allowed Eden the opportunity to concentrate on the voices coming out of the radio. She heard more shooting. *Dammit.*

"How much longer to the bank?" She yelled her question at Suzanne above the squealing tires.

"Another kilometer."

Eden flinched when more bullets exploded against their SUV.

"They're beside us," the Brit bellowed. "Speed up."

"Hold on." That was the only warning the driver gave them before he rammed the bumper into the side of the large jeep that was shooting at them.

Please God, let us get out of this alive.

"Carlson, you maniac, you'll kill us all," the fat man screeched in French.

Three people yelled *shut up* in two different languages. They might not know what he was saying, but every single person was sick of his petulant squeals.

More bullets hit their armored vehicle. Eden was pissed off when she felt herself wince again. She needed to man-up—this SUV was built like a tank, for God's sake!

Hot, sticky air suddenly suffused the interior of the Escalade. Carlson had his right arm braced over his left, his right hand holding a gun, the left on the steering wheel. Eden followed the sight of his gun and watched as he sprayed bullets into the interior of the jeep. Gusts of red plumed into the air. The jeep veered into the next lane where a tractor-trailer slammed into it.

"Fuck! Señora, how bad are you hit?" Carlson yelled.

Eden looked away from the jeep and saw blood dripping down Señora Azua's neck.

"There, on the left." The woman's voice was hoarse, but Eden could understand her. *She can't be hurt too bad, but that bleeding needs to be stopped.*

Señora Azua slumped against the front seat. "The bank is on the left." She pointed to a tall building across the meridian.

"The bank is on the left. The gates are open," Eden informed the others on the radio.

Now Señora Azua was whispering something.

"What the hell is she saying, Eden?" Carlson demanded to know.

Eden damn near crawled over the seat so she could put her ear next to Suzanne's mouth.

"Say it again," she coaxed in Spanish.

"Go up to the traffic circle," Señora Azua waved her hand at the windshield. Eden looked up ahead. With people setting up for Carnival, the zoo was already beginning to start. The driving looked like a cross between Paris and Mumbai. *We're screwed.*

"You need to go to the traffic circle to get to the bank," Eden told Carlson.

"Hold on," Carlson said again.

Eden heard the Swiss banker whimper as he clutched at his leather seat, but he didn't need to worry. The man driving their car cut off three other vehicles as he sped into the traffic circle. It was all a matter of dominance. The security specialist was supremely confident and every other driver on the road got out of his way. She just prayed that the two other members of his team following them would be as well-trained.

"Good. Good." Suzanne gasped. "There." Again, she waved weakly toward a gleaming building that was surrounded by a high security fence.

Eden looked out the rear window and saw one of the two other Escalades behind them. "Check in. I only see one of the two," Eden snapped into the radio.

"Patel here."

Then there was silence. As their driver made a shuddering right between the security gate into the bank's courtyard, he bellowed, "Rivers! Where the fuck is Rivers?!"

Eden's SUV slammed to a halt. Carlson leaned over and made a grab for the radio in Eden's hand. "Give me that." She shoved it at him.

"Rivers, check in, goddamnit." His voice oozed authority.

Nothing.

Eden opened her passenger door and Schlessinger shoved her out of the way as he dove out of the vehicle. He ended up falling to his knees. *Serves him right.* Leland Hines was coming out of the third-row seat. Eden moved back so he could get out first.

"Beauty before age," he said as he waved her toward the closed passenger door. "Let's go this way and avoid the blubbering blob, shall we?"

Whatever would get her to Suzanne the fastest was fine by Eden. She looked over the front seat and saw Carlson giving her aid, but she wanted to look over the wound. She'd learned a few things in college. It might not have been how to work on two-legged animals, but it still applied.

She jumped out the passenger door, then opened the front passenger door where Suzanne was. Out of the corner of her eye, she saw Heinrich Becker, Sharon Foster, Kaito Nakamura, and Professor Nilsson all pile out of Patel's Escalade.

She ran over to the group. "Sharon, I need your pashmina." At least she had asked before ripping it off the woman's shoulders.

The woman was pale and looked frightened to death.

"What?" she whispered. "What's going on? I don't

understand. Why were people shooting at us? Are we going to die?"

Eden saw all of the people who'd been in the vehicle with Sharon looking at the woman with various expressions of disgust or pity. Apparently, she had been the group's "Schlessinger."

"Sharon, Señora Azua is injured. I need something to stop the bleeding so we can get her into the bank. Give me your pashmina." She watched as Patel peeled away from the group to talk to a couple of men from the bank. She turned her attention back to Sharon who was still clutching the wrap around her shoulders.

"Give it to her," Heinrich Becker commanded. Sharon's hands reluctantly loosened and finally, she gave it to Eden. She then ran back to her Escalade.

"Eden, explain this to me," Schlessinger practically screamed in French from where he was sitting on the ground propped up against one of the SUV's tires. She ignored him and bent into the front seat to see Carlson with his t-shirt off trying to staunch the bleeding.

"Move," Eden said. "I need to see what we have here."

"Are you a medic?"

"I have some training," Eden prevaricated.

"It's just a flesh wound," Carlson explained. "Didn't hit anything major."

"I'm fine," Suzanne insisted.

She didn't sound fine.

Eden pulled back Carlson's shirt. All it was doing was applying pressure against the wound. Which, thank

God, showed that the bullet had just grazed her neck. *It could have been so much worse.*

The shirt wasn't helping much since it required someone holding it all the time, and Suzanne's arms were now getting floppy and her eyes glassy. Eden pressed the shirt back in place and nodded to Carlson to hold it again. She looked at the light blue cloth in her hand and tried tearing it. No go. She took ahold of it with her teeth and tried again.

Success.

She started tearing it into strips. Now she just had to figure out how to hold the makeshift bandage in place tightly enough without strangling the woman.

"How is the Señora?" a man asked over her shoulder.

"Who are you?" Carlson demanded to know.

"I am Hector Ruiz, I am the manager of the bank. I need to know what to do next, but if Señora Azua can't give us instructions, then I will need to take charge."

Eden snorted. *Yeah, sure, the bank manager's going to save us.* There was no way that Carlson was going to let *banker boy* take command.

"I'm fine," Señora Azua whispered. "Tell them to get the gates closed now."

Eden was the only one who heard her.

"She says she's fine, and close the gates."

Carlson yelled out in Spanish across the courtyard for the gates to be closed.

"Those are my employees, you shouldn't be telling them what to do. Since the Señora is injured, I need to be put in charge—you understand this, *si?*" He ignored Eden, focusing on Carlson.

"We just need to get shit done," Carlson growled.

Suzanne squeezed Eden's arm again and she bent to listen to her. But she just gasped for breath.

"You see? Everyone must listen to me. It is the only answer."

I hate these weasel types.

Time for some quick pushy bullshit. Eden again leaned down, and this time pretended that Suzanne had said something.

"Excuse me, Hector, but Señora Azua just said that she's the owner of this bank, and that if you pull this stunt she'll fire you when this is over with. Do you want to come over here and talk to her yourself?"

Carlson wiped his hand over his mouth. Eden knew damn good and well he was smothering a grin. She stole a glance at Suzanne. Her eyes were spitting fire at the officious little toad. He backed up a step.

"My apologies, Señora, I was only trying to assist you. Tell me what you want me to do."

Suzanne squeezed Eden's arm, and Eden bent down to listen to her.

"You and Carlson," she gasped.

"I'll be back," Eden assured her.

Leland Hines, Heinrich Becker, and Maurice Schlessinger had all descended on Carlson. Well, at least Schlessinger did—he practically fell into his arms, still a blubbering mess, demanding to know what was going on. Leland pulled him off Carlson and handed him off to the man who Eden knew as Patel. That was when she realized that the third SUV was not in the courtyard.

Ah, dammit. No! There were good people out there. Please God, say they're alive and safe.

She turned around so she could join in on the conversation. She came in when Leland Hines was talking.

"Bradshaw was positive that neither Maduro nor Guaido would come after us like this," Leland's lip curled.

"Well, he was dead wrong, wasn't he?" Carlson said with disgust. "It was the secret police all right. Hell, they were wearing their uniforms. The bastards."

"What? What is he saying?" Schlessinger demanded in French. Eden could care less; she was busy translating Carlson's Spanish into German for Heinrich Becker. But she held up her hand, holding her fingers close together indicating she'd tell him shortly.

"How bad is Señora Azua?" Becker asked in German. "This is her bank, she told us to come here, we need her leadership." Eden knew not to repeat the question in Spanish since Hector was still hanging around.

"It's a flesh wound. I think the bleeding has stopped, but she's hard to understand, and she needs rest. But trust me, she has all of her faculties, and we don't need that self-important bank manager trying to take charge."

Becker gave a sharp nod of agreement. "Speak for her. You know what she would say. You've been translating for all of us for weeks now. You have common sense. When it comes to the schematics of the bank, we'll figure it out."

"Eden?" Maurice Schlessinger grabbed at her arm, pitching her sideways.

"Stop! Release her at once." Becker commanded in French. It was the first time Eden had heard him speak French. He'd been holding out. She couldn't blame him—who in the hell really wanted to talk to Maurice if they didn't have to?

In halting Spanish, Heinrich Becker addressed the rest of the people in the circle. "Leland, you and Carlson go with Hector and find out where we can set up in the bank."

Carlson and Leland flanked Hector and marched him toward the entrance. Both men were peppering him with questions about the number of guards and clerical employees currently on-site.

Becker continued to ignore the pouting Schlessinger and motioned the other member of Nomad Security away from his SUV. Patel jogged over, leaving three other members of the banking contingent.

"Eden, translate."

She nodded.

"Patel, I need for you to take control of all the bank guards. I want to know exactly how many there are, and I want all weapons accounted for."

"They also have an armory on-site," Eden explained to both men. "Come here, and I'll let the Señora explain." She led them back to where Suzanne was sitting in the SUV and found her sleeping.

Damn.

"Eden, you have first aid skills, right?"

She nodded. "I'm the one who applied the bandage."

"Great, I want you to stick with the Señora."

"What about Dr. Nilsson?" Patel asked.

"She's a professor of economics." Becker was impatient with the question. "Go find Hector." After Patel left, he turned back to Eden. "I'm depending on you to get as much information as you can from Señora Azua. Got it?"

Eden nodded.

CHAPTER 4

The heavy gate opened up to a drive.

A drive that curved to a terra-cotta colored hacienda with sweeping arches covered with red and purple bougainvillea. A striking pregnant woman was waiting for them at the top of a grand staircase leading up to the front door.

Kane was the first one out of the back of the truck, followed by Max and Ezio. They had their weapons drawn. Asher saw them both reconnoiter the area and then Kane motioned for the rest of them to come out. While everybody evaluated Leo's mobility, Ash lowered himself out of the truck instead of jumping. His head wouldn't take the jarring.

Dammit, stop being a pussy!

"I heard that," Cullen said as he sidled up next to him.

"Bullshit, I didn't say anything," Asher gave his friend a wan smile.

"You were beating yourself up and calling yourself names. If I had to guess, you just called yourself a pussy," Cullen laughed at him.

It sucked having worked with the same people so damn long.

Raiden came up and handed him another mint. "I like Raiden better than you," Asher grumbled as he popped the mint in his mouth and glared at Cullen. Raiden thrust the can at Asher with a head tilt.

"Thanks," Asher said as he slid the tin of mints into his vest.

Kane jogged to the front of the truck to help Lenora Azua from the passenger seat. She was looking a damn sight better than how Asher was feeling. It had taken longer than they'd all wanted to get to her house because the streets were already beginning to fill up for the night's festivities. They had all agreed that the confusion of Carnival could work to their advantage to get past the President's secret police force and free the finance coalition from the Central Bank, then get them to the airport.

"*Abuela*," the pregnant woman called out to the older lady. "We have news since we last talked."

"Good or bad?" the old woman demanded to know.

"You need to stay calm," the pregnant woman said soothingly. "The doctor has said stress isn't good for you. He would have been angry if he'd known you were gallivanting all over the forest rescuing Americans."

Rescuing?

"I'm not the one who should be resting, it's you,

Cynthia. Get inside. Where's Rafa?" Lenora started up the steps, and Cynthia rushed down to meet her.

It was an accident waiting to happen as the old woman and the pregnant lady turned to make their way up the stairs. Cullen and Raiden followed closely in case they fell.

"Rafa is inside trying to talk to Mama."

It took a minute for Asher to make sense of it all. He was fine understanding the Spanish, just not with everybody's place in the family food chain. Suzanne Azua, the woman at the bank, must be the pregnant woman's mother, and Lenora, the old woman who had driven the truck, was Cynthia's grandmother.

He looked over at Cullen and saw that he had just done the math as well. Kane, meanwhile, was looking down at his tablet. He probably had the entire Azua family tree pulled up, and knew all of their ages, middle names, eye color, and favorite foods.

"Has anything new happened?" Lenora asked her granddaughter.

"I need you to stay calm, can you do that?" Cynthia asked when they got to the top of the stairs.

"Just tell me, child."

"Mama has a slight injury. She tells me she is fine, but she's having some trouble talking. Sometimes, the translator is helping us to understand her over the phone. There is one saving grace, and that's now she's at our bank, not the Central Bank."

"What do you mean she's at *our* bank, Señora?" Max interrupted.

A gangly teen shot out of the front door.

"Whoa, hold up." The kid raised his hands as eight guns were pointed in his direction.

The old lady jumped—as well as an old lady was able to—in front of the boy. "Put your guns down, this is Suzanne's sister's son, my grandson Rafa. He's harmless."

"Tia, I'm not harmless," the kid lamented. "That's the last time I arrange wheels for you."

"He is harmless and lacks common sense, but my grand-nephew is brilliant with computers." She patted his head.

"You guys are American Special Forces, right? What branch? Delta? Raiders? SEALs?" The kid was jazzed.

"What's your name?" Max asked with a blank face.

"Rafael Azua," Kane answered for him. "He's good, he's the nephew. Real hustler. He owns the food truck. Just turned sixteen," Kane said, looking up from his tablet. "He's already got a record with Maduro's men."

"Explain," Max demanded.

"They brought him in for questioning on their system being hacked. Because of his aunt's pull, he got out before the questioning began getting intense."

"Jesus, how old were you kid?" Max asked.

Rafa had paled. Cynthia had stood on the other side of the young man when Max started grilling him. But when that incident was brought up, her expression changed. She slapped Rafa on the back of the head.

"Hey, what's that for?" he gave her a disgruntled look.

"You could have gotten yourself killed. It didn't matter that you were twelve. They would have tortured and killed you if it hadn't been for Mama. You remember to be good."

"Fine," he gave a long-suffering sigh as he rubbed the back of his head. "But they're going to need me. You know that."

She shook her head in exasperation as she looked at Asher's team. "Come inside, gentlemen. Rafa's right, he's been talking to Mom and the translator, getting information together. It should help."

Max motioned for them to lower their weapons. Asher glanced over at Kane—he was looking at Rafa with interest. "What kind of information, kid?"

"I have everything," the teenager boasted. "I downloaded a ton of stuff from Tia Suzanne's bank after she gave me her computer code." He rubbed his hands together. "Do you know much about computers?" he asked Kane.

"A little," Kane answered.

Asher kept his laugh inside, but Cullen laughed out loud. Max sent him a sharp look. Rafa was oblivious, but Lenora didn't miss a trick.

"Well, after I got her code, I was able to get into everybody else's computer in the bank. That included IT, security, and maintenance. We won't even need access to keycards to get in because we can override the locks. Except for the gate surrounding the bank, but I'll figure out something." Kane smiled at Cynthia and Lenora as he fell into step with Rafa to enter the house. The last thing Asher heard was Rafa saying, "...otherwise the bank's security sucks donkey balls if you know what you're doing."

Now the kid was sounding like a cross between Cullen and Kane. Even Max was laughing at that. Everybody but Nic, that was. He was going to have to bone up on his Spanish.

"We need to get your mother back on the phone," Lenora said to her granddaughter as she put a comforting hand on the pregnant woman's lower back.

"The President's secret police are butchers, *Abuela*. I don't understand why they haven't broken in and killed them." The pretty young woman's voice was trembling.

"Honey, they won't. Your mother and her friends are too important. It would cause an international incident," Lenora assured the scared woman as they made their way inside.

Asher wished that was true. Cynthia was right, they were butchers. The President's secret police had been recruited from many of the deadliest street gangs in all of Columbia and Venezuela. They had no regard for human life. They needed intel from Carter from CIA, and Kane better be getting it quick. As it was, everything going on here on the ground was so fluid it felt like they were in the middle of a flood. It was making his head hurt worse than it had been when he was riding in that blasted food truck.

Asher looked around the great room the women led them into. It was huge. These people definitely had money. Of course, if Lenora's daughter owned a bank, what else could he expect?

"Where's Marta?" Lenora asked Cynthia as she looked around the room.

"I told her to take the day off," Cynthia said. "We didn't want anyone here but family when the Americans arrived. Don't worry, I've already made refreshments. They're in the fridge, I'll go get them."

Asher saw the sheen of perspiration on the pregnant woman's forehead as she took a step toward a hallway. Nic, Raiden, Cullen, and Max all began talking at once. They were volunteering to get the food if she would just tell them what to get, and Cullen coaxed her into a large plush chair. Lenora laughed.

Great, I totally missed the mark on that one. This head injury must be worse than I thought.

"Nic, you and Raiden go get the food, and bring back ice for Leo," Max directed. "Asher get over there with Kane. I want you checking out the entry points of the bank. Cullen, go park the truck around back so that it can't be seen from the road."

"The gate is very high, it should be fine," Lenora Azua assured Max. Max gave a chin tilt to Cullen, who then left to go do what Max had requested.

"Señora, I'm sure it will be fine, but I'm just the overly cautious type. Ezio, when Cullen's done parking the truck, I want the two of you to scour the outside perimeter and report back. I want to make sure that everything is as secure as it seems."

Ezio nodded and went after Cullen.

Asher started over to the other corner in the room where there was a huge monitor. Two laptops and papers piled precariously on every other remaining flat surface. Rafa was pointing at something and Kane was nodding.

"Asher, wait a minute, what's your status?" Max asked. Asher stopped mid-stride.

"I'm fine," Leo said.

"Is your name Asher?" Max growled. "If not, sit your ass down, put your leg up, and shut the hell up." Leo planted himself on one of the two sofas in the great room, and Kane absently kicked over an ottoman from where he was sitting next to Rafa so that Leo could prop up his leg.

"Now, Asher Thorne, answer me, how are you doing?" Max looked closely at Ash.

"The headache comes and goes. It's a mild concussion. I'm going to cut out video games for a while—too many blinky lights will probably aggravate the symptoms."

"Smartass," Leo said from his position on the couch. "I bet it's worse than it is, Lieutenant."

Max ignored him. He gave Asher one more hard look.

"Serious, Lieutenant, I won't put the team in danger. If it's a problem, I'll be the first to bench myself."

Max's lip ticked up into a half-smile. Which was really saying something. Then he dropped his hand on Asher's shoulder. "I know I can count on you, Ash. I need you, but only if you can perform." He gave a head tilt toward the computers, and Ash continued over to look over Kane's shoulder.

Shit, the kid really *was* good. Besides the floorplans, he had the electrical *and* the security system. But Ash saw immediately what Rafa meant about security sucking. Yeah, the gates might be reinforced steel all along the perimeter, but it didn't go deep enough into the foundation. Anyone with a little bit of C-4 and a willingness to crawl could easily break in.

All he had to do was point on the screen and Kane nodded.

"Let's just hope that the secret police force is lazy."

"What? What are you seeing?" the kid asked.

"We need to call your aunt," Asher said without answering his question. "We need to find out what the situation is like on the inside."

Raiden and Nic came in carrying some food that they passed out to everyone assembled around the room.

"Kid, call from your phone," Asher said. "Then we'll arrange something more secure."

He dialed and set his phone down on the table and put it on speaker.

A strong, self-assured woman's voice answered. She had an American accent. "Rafael, are they there?"

"How's my aunt?"

"Who's this?" Asher asked.

"I'm Eden York. Your aunt is doing pretty good, don't worry. Her throat is swollen, so she's writing things down for me."

"We can't talk on this line," Rafa said without giving anything away. "Somebody else is going to give you some instructions, okay?"

"Yes," came her immediate reply.

"Ma'am, I need you to work with someone who has a

phone that isn't being tracked. When you find that person, call back this number. We'll take it from there."

"Won't they track it once they call Rafael's phone?"

"We'll take care of things," Asher assured her.

"Okay. Give me a few minutes, and it will be done." She hung up. Asher liked her. No fuss, no muss, just down to business.

Raiden and Nic came back with a second load of empanadas and succulent shrimp wrapped in corn pancakes. Now that his head wasn't hurting as much and his stomach had calmed down, Asher was starving, and he was ready for more. Raiden must have read his mind, or heard his stomach growling, because he shoved a plate into Asher's hands.

"Eat."

Raiden then pushed another glass of ice water his way. "Drink."

"Yes, Mom."

Leo snickered up until the point that Raiden crouched down to check his knee and started whispering to him. At that point, all humor left Leo's face. Asher knew what was coming. Max strolled over to where the two of them were talking, and then he called Kane over. Yep, Leo had just been benched, and he was hating life.

Leo was not someone who stayed behind the scenes and did coordination, he was the jump-out-of-the-seat-early action dude, which is what got him in this predicament in the first place. Now he was going to have to stay behind and man the fort.

He got up from the couch and attempted to walk

without a limp to the table. He did a pretty good job but fooled no one. He sat down between Asher and Rafa, and Kane stood behind the three of them. Rafa started pointing out things to him on his computer. Leo mustered up some fake enthusiasm.

Rafa's phone rang. Asher answered it. "Answer the next call that comes in." Then hung up.

He called out from his satellite phone and put it on speaker.

"Who am I speaking to?"

"Mike Carlson. I'm one of the Senior Specialists with Nomad Security. Señora Azua, Eden, Heinrich Becker and I have the phone in a private area. Who are you?"

"I'm Asher Thorne, Petty Officer First Class of the United States Navy. You have an entire team of SEALs here. What's the situation?"

"We have ten civilians here at the bank. That includes Señora Azua who is wounded." Carlson answered.

"How bad?" Kane clipped out the question.

"A bullet zinged her across the neck," Eden jumped in. "No internal damage, but she's hurting and it's beginning to bruise around the wound. I've got ice on it, so it doesn't swell any more than it has, I want to make sure her airway stays clear."

"Have you checked down her throat?" Kane asked.

"Yes."

"What kind of background do you have? Medic?" Kane continued to drill her.

Here it goes. I hope she's not a screw-up, cause Kane will eat her for breakfast.

"A year of school that dealt specifically with animals. This included anatomy, physiology, and first aid. Let's not forget I was the one on my father's ranch who patched people up. I've got this."

"Besides pray, what are you going to do if her throat swells up and she can't breathe?" Kane asked skeptically.

"I'll just have to do a tracheotomy, now won't I?"

"A lot of cows have needed those, have they?"

"No, but I watched Grey's Anatomy a bunch of times, doesn't that count?" She didn't wait for him to answer. "Look, don't be an asshole. I will not let her die, I will get done what needs doing. I'll YouTube what I need to, or I figure one of you very capable SEALs will walk me through the procedure. Are we done here?"

"Okay, sounds like you have it covered as well as you can," Kane relented.

"Carlson, this is Asher again. How many non-civilians do you have with you?"

"There's me and one other man from Nomad Security, then there are four bank guards. Before you ask, we have plenty of firepower. They were worried about the zombie apocalypse, so they acquired an armory. And I'm not kidding."

"About the zombies, or the armory?" Ash wanted to know.

"Carlson, you're out of line," Eden cut in. "With the gangs around here, it's been like the wild west, and who in the hell was the Señora going to depend on, the secret police? She wasn't just protecting the assets of this bank, she was protecting each and every one of her employees."

There was a long pause.

"She wrote all of that out?" Asher asked.

"She didn't have to; anyone with two brain cells to rub together would know what was up. And by the way, she has just written down that Carlson is an asshole and that I was right."

From across the room, Lenora and Cynthia's laughter joined Rafa's.

"Seriously, you don't want to mess with my aunt. She will cut you up." Rafa said.

"Sounds like Eden will, too," Asher muttered.

"Now that the armory has been explained, let me tell you about the people we've lost." Carlson's voice was subdued. "My man was driving three other members of the financial contingent. We couldn't get anyone to respond via cell or radio, then there was a report on the police band radio of a black SUV that was in a bad wreck with no survivors. We have to assume that's ours. That could be a smokescreen. We could have people who have been taken by the secret police."

Asher heard a woman gasp. *Was that Eden?*

"How did that happen?" Asher asked.

"Patel said Rivers' SUV had their tires shot out by the secret police. When he turned around to get them, their car had been rammed. He couldn't stick around."

"Is there anything else?" Asher asked.

A man answered with a distinct German accent. "I have been in contact with my Chancellor and she assures me that all of the Western allies have been in contact with the American government and have our own special forces members ready to work with you if that is required."

Asher winced. The idea of having international teams of Spec Ops descending on Caracas made him cringe, and when he looked around the room, he saw that everybody else was feeling the same way. What was worse, they all knew damn good and well that his call had been monitored by Madura's men.

Great, just fucking great.

"Is this Heinrich Becker?" Max asked.

"Yes, I'm the head of the IMF," he answered. "And you are?"

"I'm Lieutenant Max Hogan of the United States Navy SEAL Team. Myself and six of my men will extract you from the bank and take you to the airport where a plane will be waiting. You will then be transported to Puerto Rico."

"What about my six bank employees?" Señora Azua whispered in a harsh voice, then she started to cough. There was a long pause.

"She's right, Lieutenant Hogan. Are you planning on pulling these people out of Venezuela? What about their families, are you taking them as well? Have you thought this through?" Eden wasn't strident, she was calmly asking questions on behalf of Suzanne Azua, making sure she was acting in the woman's best interests.

Max ran his hand through his close-cropped hair.

"One of my men is going to make sure that Señora

Azua gets the care she needs. That will be priority number one. Her being here in Venezuela will be natural. As for the other bank employees, they can come here to the Azua hacienda and leave at different times, so that they get home safely."

"How will you accomplish this?" Eden persisted.

"We just will," Asher jumped in. "It's our job."

"But—"

"Eden, you gotta trust us, we know what we're doing. Can you do that?"

Another long pause.

"It goes against my nature, but I've got to believe in something. This is a shitstorm. Please just make sure you come through for these people. Please."

CHAPTER 5

Leland clapped his hand on Eden's shoulder after the line was disconnected. "They're good. I might not know these men in particular, but I've served with SEALs before, and I believe in them. They'll come through, just watch."

Eden was able to muster up a fake smile. Blindly believe in her dad? Her brothers? Hell, even Lori or Jenny, absolutely. But these guys? *Hell, no.* It was up to her and whoever else she deemed worth a damn.

After Leland turned to talk to the other two men, Eden looked around the room to see who else might have half a brain cell during a crisis. Carlson was a definite yes, despite the fact his boss was a sniveling weasel who had abandoned everybody and headed for Aruba. Probably Patel. The bank guards? Too soon to tell. Leland with his military background sounded good… She closed her eyes and pressed her fingers to the bridge of her nose, trying to relieve the pressure building up in her sinuses.

Suzanne, who was resting against the arm of the couch beside Eden, tugged at Eden's sleeve. She glanced up and saw that the men were deep in conversation. When she turned back to Suzanne, the woman made a gesture with her hand indicating she didn't want them involved.

Curious.

Eden scooched over so she could hear Suzanne.

"I," Suzanne started to cough. Eden looked at her and noted that blood was seeping through the sky-blue pashmina.

Dammit!

"Use the notepad, Señora." She nodded to the pad of paper Suzanne had grabbed from her purse.

The woman started to shake her head in defiance and more blood seeped. She let out a slight moan of pain, not enough to get the men's attention, but enough for Eden's eyes to light up.

Suzanne held up her hand to ward off the admonishment she was about to receive, and instead picked up the notepad and a pen.

Tear this up after you've read it, she wrote in Spanish.

Eden nodded.

In the car, before I was shot, I texted my bank security passwords to my nephew. He's a hacker. He'll help the SEAL team to get into the bank.

Eden took the written page, folded it, and put it in her skirt's little pocket. Then she bent close to Señora Azua's ear. In an almost non-existent whisper, she asked, "Why didn't you say this in front of the men?"

I don't trust Becker or Carlson.

Eden closed her eyes and prayed for strength. *Really? We have a traitor in our midst? What the hell?* That made no sense, why would anyone be on Maduro's payroll? What could possibly be in it for them?

She took the paper the Señora had written on and shoved it next to the other piece of paper.

Eden made sure the men were still not looking at them, then whispered to Suzanne again. "Why wouldn't you trust them?"

Too many things went wrong while the Nomad Security Company was in charge. Becker hasn't been working in Venezuela's best interests during meetings. It's almost as if he has investments with Maduro.

Holy shit! That put an entirely different spin on a meeting she had translated between Becker, Dr. Nilsson, and the head of the Central bank.

Looking at the men out of the corner of her eye, Eden skipped the pocket of her skirt and actually shoved *that* piece of paper inside her bra, which was deeper than her pockets.

"Leland?" Eden whispered.

Suzanne gave her a thumbs up.

Thank God. She really liked the man and had been counting on him as an asset.

"Hector?"

Suzanne rolled her eyes, then wrote on her notepad.

He's useless. Guards are good. See if Torres is here. He's excellent.

The woman slumped back onto the arm of the sofa.

She was spent. So was Eden. *What the hell? Two possible traitors?* There they were, the three of them, acting like fraternity buddies. All the time she'd been pretty sure Becker had known French and had been pleading ignorance so he could get out of talking to Schlessinger, but she'd never guessed that he'd had this much of a grasp of Spanish. Definitely not enough for the three of them to be conversing in it. *How could I have missed all of those red flags?*

Suzanne grasped Eden's hair and pulled her head down so she could whisper in her ear. "Family emergency code word is *burning*."

Suzanne's eyes fluttered closed and she slowly slid sideways against the back cushion of the couch.

Dammit. What did that mean? Code word? *Sure, I had a code word with Jenny and Lori when we were ten, but the Azua's have one now? What the hell?*

Eden grasped her hand and Suzanne gave a slight squeeze. Then she gestured for Eden to come close again. "I told you, no talking," Eden whispered vehemently.

"Is Señora Azua okay?" Carlson asked.

"She's conscious. Just tired. I think rest is the best thing for her."

Leland got up from his chair and towered over the sofa. "Do you mind?" motioning for Eden to get out of the way. "I'm going to reposition her." He gently picked Suzanne up into his arms.

Eden snagged the two decorative pillows from the couch and placed them at one end so that he could lie her down in a more comfortable position. After he was done, she watched as he took off his suit jacket and laid it over the woman.

Before she had a chance to say anything else, she saw Schlessinger barreling into Azua's private office. *Great.*

"What's going on?" he demanded in French.

The three men looked at her, as if answering him was her problem.

"Monsieur Becker can explain. I need to find the first aid kit for Senor Azua," she said as she brushed past the obnoxious man.

She heard Becker's sigh as she left the room. *Serves him right.*

Asher sucked down another glass of water with some Tylenol. Thank God the jackhammer in his head had toned down to just a bongo drum. It made it easy enough for him to really assess where the bank gate was the most vulnerable. Rafa was right; once they got past the gate, maneuvering around the building would be easy with the security codes that he'd been provided. Still, how to get into the gate without alerting the secret police—that was the problem.

"It's got to be done here at the southwest corner," Kane said for the fourth time. His voice was seriously beginning to grate on Asher's last nerve. He loved Kane, but the man didn't know explosives like he did.

"Kane, it is definitely more vulnerable there, but everybody and their brother will see what we're doing. If we set the charges, here, here, and here," Asher pointed at the three different stress points clustered together behind the building, "we can get the same effect."

"Yeah, but the odds of getting it just right are astronomical."

Asher shot Kane a disparaging look. "Do I go about doubting your computer geeky expertise? No. I just assume that somewhere, sometime, you ate a bunch of computer parts as a child and you are now part cyborg. Just quit second-guessing me and let me do my job."

Kane gave him a humble look. "First, I'm not a cyborg."

"No, he's an android," Cullen spoke up.

"Second, I'm sorry. Totally out of line."

"Yep, you were," Cullen chimed in.

Both Asher and Kane said *shut up* at the same time. Cullen laughed.

"But even after you do your magic—which of course you will because you are exceptionally good at your job—we still need to keep the secret police off our ass. That requires a diversion," Cullen reminded them.

"You mean something that includes an alligator?" Asher asked Cullen.

"Nah, something with a little more bite," Cullen grinned.

Asher noticed Rafa watching them all talk, with a confused look on his face. Asher realized that even though the kid knew some English, this was going way over his head. What was worse, Leo was being left out. *Not good.*

"Leo, you're in charge of figuring out the diversion. Use Cullen's experience as a professional dumbass to see what you can come up with."

"Leo, my services are at your disposal," Cullen dipped his head with a grin. "First, we have to decide what costumes we want to wear to mingle in with the other people at Carnival."

"Oh God, my headache is getting worse," Ash complained. "Time to leave you to it," he got up from his chair. He and Kane headed over to Max.

"Did anything new come in from Carter at CIA?" Max asked as he stepped away from the Azua women.

Kane shook his head. "He's been silent for the last hour since I told him we have all the details on the bank. He's pissed as hell that Bradshaw skipped out to Aruba. Nomad Security has a pristine reputation internationally, so the fact that this happened is raising flags all over the world."

"I don't really give a shit. It happened, and we now have ten civilians whose lives are on the line, because he was stupid, greedy, or a coward. All three of those options are fucked-up in my book," Asher said heatedly.

"What Ash said." Max nodded. "You get Carter on the goddamn phone. You find out which way the wind is blowing. We have two more Nomad employees in the bank with those civilians and I don't want to find out that those people are in a henhouse with a fox. If those other two Nomad Security people are giving Maduro info, I want to know, now!"

Kane just raised his eyebrow. Ash knew what that

meant. It meant that Kane was on it, and that Carter's ass was going to be grass if he didn't get back to him. And it probably meant that—

"I got sick of waiting on him, so I have one of my less reputable friends working on this from a different angle. Him, I trust."

Asher chuckled. "Let me get this right, you trust the untrustworthy guy, but the man we're supposed to depend on?" He let his voice trail off.

"Carter's new to me. Since Isaacson got pissed-off and decided to quit, and Worthington retired, I'm nervous. So yeah, my friends who have spent their lives in the shadows are A-plus in my book."

"Yep, as long as they're working on the side of the angels, I don't care about their means and methods," Asher agreed.

Max pretended like he wasn't listening.

Must suck to be an officer.

Kane's satellite phone pinged. He looked at the display, then looked at Asher and Max and said, "nothing personal," before he walked away.

Max's jaw clenched, but that was the only outward sign that he was upset about what was going on. Asher knew he had to be seething with everything that had gone wrong, but Max Hogan would never let his team know that. Instead, he would be the rock that they could all depend on.

"Asher, I know you can open up a space into the gate, but how many can get in at a time?" Max asked.

"One. If we did it where Kane is suggesting, we could do it two at a time, no problem."

"It's not worth the risk," Max's voice was emphatic. "You have it right, we need to do it around back. You'll make it work. I want you going through first. The problem is determining who's going to meet you. I don't want Nomad personnel to be your reception party."

He'd been thinking the same thing, but how in the hell were they going to prevent that? "Let me give this a minute of thought. There has to be a way to get this accomplished without running into an ambush."

"I've got something," Kane said as he returned.

"What?" Max asked.

"Bradshaw is dead. Fucking Carter from CIA doesn't even know it yet, but there's been a fire at the Imperial Hotel on Aruba, multiple casualties and one death. It was Bradshaw's alias. We're not quite sure when it happened, but it was recent."

"So, somebody is trying to tie up some loose ends. That only makes it more likely that Nomad was on Maduro's payroll and that we can't trust Patel or Carlson," Asher surmised.

"That's my take," Kane agreed.

CHAPTER 6

Señora Azua hadn't moved much when Eden had applied a real bandage to her neck, and now she didn't even flinch when Carlson's phone rang. That really worried Eden.

"Yes," Carlson answered tersely. He looked around before putting it on speaker. Can't say she blamed him, since Schlessinger had been roosting in the office for the last hour. She wouldn't want him listening in either, not that he could understand Spanish.

"Is this Carlson?" a voice asked.

"Yes, which one are you?"

"This is Asher Thorne. I'm going to be coordinating the entry into the bank. I need to ask a few questions of Señora Azua or one of her employees, preferably one who is familiar with the building layout and security."

"How are you planning on getting into the bank? We're surrounded by Maduro's men," Carlson demanded to know.

"It's Mike, right? Mike Carlson?"

"Yes," Carlson answered slowly.

"Well, Mike. I can't rightly answer that question since I haven't spoken to the people who need to provide me with some details I need. Are you going to put them on the phone or not?"

Oh, he's good. He just shoved that knife right through Carlson's ribcage straight into his beating heart. Eden had to smother a grin at Carlson's less than happy expression.

"Señora Azua is resting. I'll get Hector, he's the bank manager," Carlson bit out.

"Actually," Eden interrupted. "I spoke to the Señora before she went to sleep. She said that we should find the guard named Torres, he would be the best one to help us get information. It sounded like Hector was more of a bureaucrat."

"Hi, Eden," Asher said.

Yay, I got a pleasant voice. Screw you, Mike. See, you catch more flies with honey than vinegar. I'm loving Carlson's pissed-off expression.

"Why didn't she tell all of us?" Carlson asked as he pointed to Leland and waved his hand toward the door where Becker was outside avoiding Schlessinger.

"She can't strain her voice," Eden explained. "What's more, the three of you were talking amongst yourselves."

"It's true, we were," Leland confirmed.

"Stay on track," Asher coached them. "I need some inside help. Get this Torres guy."

"I'll go," Eden said. She wanted a chance to see if

Chairman Becker was out whispering with Dr. Nilsson. Or worse yet, was he on his phone making calls to Maduro's men? Dammit, she needed a spy of her own to keep track of both Carlson and Becker in case one or both were bad guys.

"Hurry up," Carlson ordered.

She rolled her eyes at him and hurried out of the room. At least as fast as her pencil skirt allowed her to go.

There in one of the office cubicles, she spotted Heinrich Becker with Gerta Nilsson. She hoped that since Kaito Nakamura was with them that she was wrong, and they weren't in cahoots with Maduro. Maybe, just maybe, they weren't trying to figure out a way to sell everyone out and have the secret police smear them into the ground like roadkill.

Okay, I need to quit obsessing and focus on finding Torres. Suzanne promised me he would be excellent. And I want excellent. Asher seems excellent. Please say I'm right. Please say I'm not just spitting in the wind.

Eden saw two men coming out of the door at the far end of the open office area. One was kind of small, the other looked big and mean. She hoped that the big and mean one was Torres. She headed their way. Big and mean looked up at her and smiled.

"Hello," Eden started in Spanish. "I'm Eden York and Señora Azua has been telling me wonderful things about the guards here at her bank."

The small man frowned. "Where is the Señora?" he asked.

"She is resting in her office, she'll—"

"How badly is she injured?" the man persisted.

"Not too bad. As long as infection doesn't set in or her throat doesn't swell up, she'll be fine."

"We need to get her to the hospital." He looked over to big and mean. "Marco, I want you up on the roof. I want a count of exactly how many men, vehicles, and snipers are surrounding us. You have twenty minutes to get that report back to me."

The big and mean Marco hopped to it by immediately turning back to the door that led to the stairs, which Eden assumed led to the roof.

The guard, who clearly knew his stuff, rubbed his right temple. "Thank you for taking care of Señora Azua, she is a fine lady."

Eden held out her hand and the man took it. "I'm sorry, where are my manners?" he asked with a small smile. "My name is Angelo Torres. Normally I supervise the guards on the night shift. I volunteered to work today because it is Carnival."

Eden felt herself relax. Suzanne had been right, this was *the guy*. "How much trouble are we in?" she asked.

"A lot. I'll know more after Marco reports, but we're in for a great deal of trouble. What I don't understand is why Maduro's men haven't launched a full-on assault and just taken the Señora, you, and the other bankers. This makes no sense to me...unless."

He stroked the wispy stubble on his chin.

After waiting patiently for almost a minute, Eden lost it. "Unless what, Angelo?"

"Unless they don't have Maduro's permission. They

won't wipe their asses unless that pig gives them permission."

Eden winced at the imagery. Torres noticed it, then *he* winced.

"I beg your pardon, Senorita. This is a difficult situation, but there is never a reason to use strong language in front of a lady such as yourself."

Eden laughed. "My father is retired military and now is a sheriff in a small town. My brothers, well, let's just say they are all in different fields that take swearing for granted. I just haven't been home for a while, so you caught me off-guard."

"That is still not a reason for me to not treat you with respect. Will you forgive my lack of manners?" She could tell he was serious about this forgiveness bullshit.

She inclined her head. "Of course, you're forgiven. This is a difficult situation," she parroted back to the man. "But I would like to ask why you think that Maduro hasn't given them permission."

Again, he stroked his chin as he looked off into space, then he looked at her with laser focus. "I think that they can't get ahold of him. It is rumored that for our national holiday, President Maduro normally goes to the Isla de Margarita. I know for a fact that he has a second home under an alias on the Western tip of the Macanao Peninsula."

"I still don't get it, why not just contact him?"

"He doesn't go there with his family." The man looked uncomfortable. He finally answered. "He is usually there with one or more ladies of ill-repute."

Eden had to stop herself from rolling her eyes at the way Torres tried to spare her sensibilities. Truly, she didn't think any man had ever worried about her more than this guy. It might be cute, but it was getting on her nerves.

"Got it. I understand. So how long do we have? How long will these women keep Maduro occupied before he comes up for air?"

"I don't know. Maybe until Monday?"

The door slammed open and they both turned to look. Marco was breathing heavily. "Wait a moment," Torres said, turning back to Eden. "Maduro will definitely be back to attend mass on Sunday with his wife."

Shit.

"What time?"

"The eleven o'clock service. He likes to sleep in."

It was now early Friday afternoon and people were pouring into the street to get ready for Carnival. It was a crapshoot if Maduro would be commanding his men on Saturday night, or Sunday morning, but those goddamn SEALs better be on the ball.

"Senor Torres, I need you to come with me," she said. "You need to give some information to some people who can help us."

"First, I need Marco to give me *his* report."

Eden listened. It was bad. Really bad.

"How in the hell are we going to get Carlson off the damn phone?" Leo asked.

Asher looked over his shoulder at the man. Subterfuge was not one of Leo's strong points—he went in with both guns blazing every fricking time. Asher loved having his friend watch his back, but when they needed to talk their way out of a fight, Leo was not the guy you wanted at your side.

"With finesse, and Asher can do it. He's almost as good as Kane," Cullen assured Leo.

"I resent that. Kane's so busy running background checks on everybody, he's forgotten the fine art of diplomacy and subtlety."

"If you have enough information, you don't have to wait around for folks to fess up, you already know everything," Kane smirked as he and Cullen stood over Rafa, Asher, and Leo as they looked at the schematics of the bank.

"How's that 'knowing everything' working for you in your life with A.J.?" Cullen asked.

"Shut up," Kane said without heat.

Asher held up his hand to gather some control. "Let's make another call. I'll wing it, and see if I can get Heinrich Becker, Leland Hines, or Eden York to take over the call and send Carlson on some fool's errand."

Leo snorted. "Good luck with that, Mr. Diplomat."

They're bringing my headache back.

He looked across the room to where Raiden, Nic, Ezio, and Max were huddled together. He knew that they were figuring out transportation that didn't include a food truck, as well as the best routes to the hospital, hacienda, and airport. He caught Raiden's eye. Soon, Raiden had two ice packs in his hands and was providing them to Asher and Leo.

When Leo looked like he was going to protest, Raiden told him to suck it up. Asher just took his with grateful dignity and placed it against his throbbing head.

"What can I do?" Rafa asked. Asher wasn't surprised; the kid had been chomping at the bit to get back in the action for the last forty-five minutes. Couldn't blame him since it was his family on the line.

"Make the call," Asher said. "Let's see if your aunt is feeling better. Maybe we can get her to talk this time."

Asher wasn't hopeful, but he wasn't going to tell that to the kid. He watched as Rafa punched in the number. Carlson immediately answered the phone.

"Is this Thorne?" He did not sound happy.

Asher smiled. *Glad to see I made a good impression.* He didn't say anything, allowing the kid to speak.

"Can I talk to my aunt?"

"Who's this?" Again, Carlson was a surly bastard. *Who pissed in his Cheerios? Did he have to be a prick to a teenager who was worried about his aunt?*

"That's Rafael Azua, he's Suzanne Azua's nephew. He wants to know if she's okay. Is she?" Asher bit out the question.

"Look, we don't have time for that. She's going to make it. We need to coordinate—"

"This is Eden. Your aunt is resting. This is Rafa, right?"

"Yes, Señora. She's really going to be all right?" There was a tremble in his voice.

"I promise you, she will be fine. I would worry if she were burning up with fever, but she's not."

Instead of answering her, the kid's head shot up and he looked at Asher with wide eyes. *What the hell is that about? The kid should be happy his aunt is fine. What's going on here?*

Asher decided to step in. "Eden, we have a few ideas on how we're going to get into the bank without alerting Maduro's men."

"What are your plans?" Carlson demanded to know.

"They're fluid right now. Currently, we're trying to get a take on the number of people that Maduro has surrounding the bank."

"I have that number," Eden said. "Or I should say, Angelo Torres does. He is the lead guard here at the bank." Asher really liked her delivery. She was cool as a cucumber. Now if he could just find a way to talk to her without Carlson around.

Rafa covered the mouthpiece of the satellite phone and gave Asher a determined look. "There is something wrong. Señora York used the code word."

"What?"

"She used my aunt's emergency code word. She said *burning*. Our family was supposed to use that word if any of us ever got into trouble. Like a robber came into the house or something."

Ah. Must be why he looked so upset. But was he right? Asher thought through Eden's sentence. There was really no reason for her to have said burning up with fever. But if the kid was right, then she knew things were hinky on her end, *and Hallelujah for that!* Now, to somehow use it to their advantage.

Maybe....

"How much juice on the phone you're using?" Asher quickly asked.

"I'm at forty-two percent," Carlson answered.

"Do you have a charger?"

"No," the man reluctantly admitted.

"We're going to need some back-up phones to communicate from. I'm going to give you this number, and someone needs to go and see which phones have the capability to dial out to this number. Then bring all of those phones into wherever you are."

"I'll also check desks to see if any of the bank employees left behind chargers," Eden volunteered. "It'll take more than a minute though."

"This is important. Take as long as you need," Asher responded. *Please God, say that there's a family code word, and she understood what I was saying.* He needed to talk to her away from Carlson.

"Okay, I'm going to go see what I can find," Eden said.

"Yeah, yeah, do whatever," Carlson bellowed. "Meanwhile, this guy can fill me in on what kind of plan him and his team have come up with."

"No. First, Torres is going to tell me what he found out about the number of men who are surrounding the bank," Ash answered.

A new voice spoke up. "There are five jeeps with long-range mounted machine guns. From what my man could see, there are at least three men with RPGs. Our reinforced gate couldn't withstand two grenade shots at the same spot. But I don't think the secret police would want to risk that. It would mean that within minutes, the entire city would know that the secret police were mounting an all-out assault on the bank. Maduro would have to come up with quite the story to explain away why he approved that."

Shit. RPGs, long-range machine guns. We are so fucked.

Asher looked over at Leo and Kane—they looked as grim as he felt.

"What the hell are you going to do about this?" Carlson demanded.

"Excuse me, what was the other gentleman's name? Was that Senor Torres?" Asher asked calmly.

"Yes, I am Angelo Torres. I manage the guards here at night. I have worked at Banco de la Gente for the last seventeen years," he said proudly. "Señorita York has explained things to me, but I still do not understand how you Americans are going to help us."

"That makes two of us," Carlson spat out. "Thorne, you heard the man, there's an army out there. What in the hell are you planning?"

"Torres, is that all your man told you?"

"No, there is more. The good news is that we are the tallest building for blocks, but there are snipers on other nearby low buildings that are targeting our courtyard. We don't have anyone there for the time being, but one of the safety precautions when this building was built, is that there is at least a six-foot perimeter between the building and the gate."

"We have the specs, Angelo. But even with the six feet, there are some angles that are going to be almost impossible for Maduro's men to get off a shot, aren't there?" Leo asked.

Asher nodded. Leo was seeing things exactly right as they looked at the blueprints up on Rafa's screen. Especially at the corners—there wasn't a chance in hell that Maduro's snipers could make that shot.

"You're right," Torres finally spoke up. "I need to get up on our roof and check things out myself. Then I'll be able to give you positions of the jeeps and snipers."

"That would be perfect. How soon do you think you could have that for us? Can you draw us a map?" Asher asked.

As Torres started to answer, there was an incoming call. It was a US area code he didn't recognize. He held it up to Kane.

"Montana," he mouthed.

Jackpot!

"Carlson, we have an urgent call from one of our contacts that we have to take. We'll get back to you as soon as possible."

"But—"

"Later," Asher said as he hung up on the man.

Asher watched as Kane walked over to brief Max, Ezio, Nic, and Raiden on the information that Torres had provided. They were going to need that to figure out if there was any way to debilitate or sabotage the jeeps and snipers.

He switched over to the other line.

"Hello?"

"This is Eden York. Asher, right?"

"Yes, ma'am."

"Thank God, the code word worked. I guess Rafa is with you."

"Yes! How's Aunt Suzanne? Is she okay?" Rafa interjected. He was clearly upset.

"She's going to be just fine." Her voice was low and calm for the young man.

"Are you telling me the truth, or just what you want me to hear?"

"I wouldn't do that to you. Your aunt has put her trust in you, Rafa, and she has told me that you have a good head on your shoulders and that you're going to be helping the Americans get in here and rescue us."

Asher watched as the kid preened. *Damn, she's good at this.*

"Can I talk to her?" Rafa asked.

"I'm talking in the women's bathroom. It's the only place I could think of that Carlson and Becker wouldn't be able to hear me. But I'm worried that Dr. Nilsson might be in on this, too. I don't know who we can trust at this point."

"Becker? You think that Becker might be a mole for Maduro?" Asher asked. That changed everything. If they had two potential bad guys, they were in a world of hurt.

"Suzanne slipped me some notes while the men were occupied. She said that Becker was doing some hinky things with his investments. It looked like he might be busy feathering his nest with money from Maduro."

"Asshole," Asher breathed.

"What are you talking about?" Cullen said over his shoulder. "That's one twisted asshole. You're telling me one of the guys who is supposed to be doing good in the world is actually helping to steal from starving people? There is a special place in hell for that type of motherfucker."

"You got that right," Eden said with feeling. Asher cracked a smile. *She's a bloodthirsty little thing.* He liked it. "But," she started, "so far, we only have a theory. Suzanne needs to wake up and fill us in more on what she saw and heard. It would be great if someone could follow that bastard's money. That is not my forte."

"But you work for the International Money Fund, aren't you some kind of accounting genius?" Cullen asked.

"She's a translator," Asher answered. "She's a genius in languages. According to her file, she speaks six different ones fluently."

"Seven," Eden said. "But who's counting? Look, the other problem we have is Carlson. Suzanne didn't explain why she didn't trust him, just that she didn't. I figure it had to do with his boss leaving us high and dry as he flew off to Aruba. What a pissant." Her voice dripped with disgust.

"Yeah, the entire Special Operations Forces

community has gone batshit crazy over the Nomad situation. They can't believe that Bradshaw left you hanging like that. Everybody wants to know if the entire Nomad team in Venezuela has been compromised."

"The Señora only mentioned Carlson, but if he's under the microscope, I have to assume Patel could be rogue, too," Eden agreed.

"Lyons, quit with the bullshit and get over here. We need to talk about the intel that Kane just shared," Max called from across the room.

Cullen rubbed his hands in anticipation and double-timed it over to the small group. Asher turned his attention back to Eden. "You're right to be wary of Patel. We have someone doing checks on both of them. Now that you gave us Becker's name, he'll follow the money."

"I don't see how. He's a banker, for God's sake. If anybody can hide money, it's him."

"You don't know Kane. Trust me, we'll know."

"I'll believe it when I see it."

Asher laughed. "Have trust issues much?"

Leo snorted.

"No, I trust my family implicitly. Anyone else? It takes a little bit more than a minute."

Asher winced.

"Is this going to be a problem with you helping us?" he finally asked.

"Nope. I see you as our best shot out of here. I'd have to be an idiot not to help in our rescue. With that said, don't think I'm just going to follow orders blindly. You better give me a good reason if something seems stupid."

Leo rolled his eyes.

"That's not going to be a problem, Eden. We're going to have damn good reasons for everything we ask you to do. First thing? Put your phone on vibrate. Second, do you have someplace you can conceal it on your person?"

"Yes, and yes."

"Third, check your settings, make sure that when you get a text, it only vibrates once. This will be the way we will communicate back and forth. One vibration means you have ten minutes to get back to us. Two immediate vibrations in a row means drop everything and find a way to get us on the phone. Three immediate vibrations in a row means you have one minute to duck and cover."

"And in one of our many *tête-à-têtes*, will you have appraised me of the duck and cover potential?" He heard laughter in her voice.

His lip twitched. "If all goes to plan, then yes."

"So, there is a plan?"

"One is beginning to take shape."

"That's what my brothers used to say when they were flying by the seat of their pants," Eden sighed. "But they always came out alive, so that's something."

"Count on it."

He could hear two female voices who must have just entered the bathroom. Eden hung up the phone.

CHAPTER 7

Her hands were sweaty. Not clammy. Actually sweaty. And her blouse was getting sticky because she'd been wearing it since yesterday morning, and now it was almost four o'clock Friday afternoon.

She rubbed them against her skirt and cursed Asher Thorne. It had been five hours since she'd first talked privately with Asher, and on the last phone call, he'd told her their plan. It was worse than anything her dumbass brothers had come up with in their wild, drunken, teenage years in the wilds of Montana. They were going to have to be smarter, better, and really, really lucky to pull this off.

Since her phone was stuck deep in her underwire bra, she glanced over at Carlson's phone. It was thirteen minutes to the top of the hour. Señora Azua's executive office was on the opposite side of the huge open bank area. As soon as the explosions started, she was going to need to get her down the stairway to the vault. This floor and the two below it would be toast. She needed to give Suzanne a head start.

Eden's head swiveled away from Carlson's phone to look at Suzanne's pale face. Despite the intermittent ice packs, Eden hadn't seen a discernable reduction of the swelling on her neck. She needed to be seen by a doctor, not some wanna-be-veterinarian. Eden had been giving her slow sips of water to ease the pain in her throat, and now it was time for her to pee, whether she needed to or not. The fact that the woman's bathroom was next to the stairway was just a happy coincidence.

She leaned over and put her ear near the woman's face.

"You need to use the restroom?" Eden queried. "Yeah, we can arrange that."

Suzanne's eyes fluttered open, but the woman looked at her with keen intelligence.

"Help me up," she whispered.

"Leland?" Eden turned to the man to see that he was already standing up.

"I'll help." All of his attention was focused on Suzanne.

"When the hell are those damn frogmen going to let us know what the hell is going on?" Carlson groused. He punched repeat on his phone again, trying to get Asher or anybody else on the team to answer. Eden knew it was useless, but she sure as hell wasn't going to tell him.

"Leland, she needs to walk a little bit. She's not going to want you to sit her on the toilet," Eden whispered when he went to pick Suzanne up.

"Then she can stand up when we reach the bathroom door," he said grimly.

Eden's lip twitched. The man reminded her of her dad. What the hell, when all hell broke loose, he could carry Suzanne downstairs. That would be much better than trying to help her down the stairs on her own.

She looked over at Carlson's phone. Eleven minutes.

Asher looked down at his watch. It was seventeen hours since they'd landed in Venezuela, and he was about to execute one of the most bizarre plans known to mankind, let alone a special operations force.

He just thanked God it didn't include a fucking clown car. He was sure it would have, except it was too small. No, instead, he was stuck with feathers, crepe paper, a giant dragon head, and a metric shit ton of green sateen with gold trim. He worked through the giant cut-out that they'd made in the neck of the dragon so he could work.

Turned out Ezio's grandma was addicted to Macy's Thanksgiving Day Parade. As a result, Ezio knew as much about that parade as Cullen knew about Mardi Gras. Between those two things, they came up with the idea on how to hide the explosions that Asher was going to make as he blew out a hole in the back wall. They were like two tweenyboppers talking about the hot boy at school as they figured out how they needed to steal a float and butt it up against the back gate and have Asher hide underneath it.

Then Rafa got into the game, and it became teenager central. Rafa of course knew somebody who knew somebody. Before Asher knew it, they were going to a run-down garage in the back of an auto body shop where a bunch of university students had a float they were willing to sell. All they wanted were a couple of iPhones that Rafa was able to scrape together from another deal that he cut.

Cullen was loving every moment of it. Ezio played his part, too. The girls didn't recognize one uniform from another, and Ezio was able to get the couple of University girls to swoon over his good looks, which helped the deal to go down easier for Rafa.

All three of them were crazy. Certifiable. Nuts. But they made it happen.

Now here Asher was, sweating like a dyslexic at countdown. The night was hot and humid as fuck. Add in the body armor, being wrapped in neon green material that didn't breathe, and then like a turd cherry on top, there was the paper mâché dragon's head that hovered over *his* head.

"You doing okay?" Ezio asked from behind him.

"Dandy."

"Come on, haven't you ever wanted to be in a parade?"

"No." Asher concentrated on applying the C-4 charges to the exact right pressure points on the steel gate.

Damn, it's hot.

He would have preferred doing this alone. If something went wrong, he'd like to be the only casualty—not that he intended anything to go wrong. He was damn good at this. But still, it pissed him off that Ezio was anywhere near the charges. But someone needed to help push the float along. *Why did this have to be some half-assed parade float that needed two people inside it to get it moving?*

Just one more. He wiped the sweat out of his eyes and adjusted the charge. Dammit, he blinked and realized he needed to pull out the fuse and reposition it. Finally, it was right. He blew out a long breath and checked his watch. Adjusting the timer to make sure it coordinated with the time he had supplied Eden, Asher then turned to handle the next bit of fun.

He looked around the inside of the parade float. It wasn't the sturdiest thing he'd ever seen, but since the charges were set up at the weak spots, they didn't need as much C-4 as they would other places. The float would be toast when the charges blew, but hopefully, people would just think it was a pyrotechnic display gone wrong.

A dragon. Asher shook his head. And he had thought the damn Eurovision Song Contest was the craziest mission.

"Let's move," Asher said as he pulled at Ezio's sleeve. Ezio immediately understood and moved.

As soon as they crawled out from beneath the green monstrosity, Asher took a deep breath, then looked up at the tall gate of the bank. He grinned as he saw the food truck thirty meters away. There were Rafa and two of the university girls he'd recruited giving away free plantains and empanadas, keeping civilians away from the blast site. Cullen really was a devious bastard, and Rafa fit right in. Free food was brilliant.

Meanwhile, he and Ezio slid over to where Raiden and Nic were waiting in a covered truck that they had *procured*. "Two minutes," Asher informed them. "Then I'm going in."

Raiden nodded.

"Max and Kane? Have we heard from them?" Asher asked.

"Not yet. But you know they want to be thorough," Raiden answered.

"Does Kane really think he can block any kind of communication between Maduro and his men?"

Raiden shrugged. Nic looked over at him and frowned. "He *can* do it, can't he?"

"If he thinks he can, he probably can. Problem is that some of the people he normally relies on to help him are out of the game. He hasn't been his happy-go-lucky self lately."

Raiden had that right. First, there were the two he trusted from the US Intelligence community who had quit and retired, and then to find out that the lieutenant of Midnight Delta still had his computer expert under lock and key, was pissing Kane off.

Asher looked at his watch. One and thirty seconds. He took out his satellite phone, and at precisely one minute before the charges were to blow, he quickly texted Eden three times.

Leland was looking pissed. "Why haven't you moved everyone to the basement? Why are you doing this and not Carlson? What in the hell is going on?" he demanded to know.

"I did this as a precaution only. Nobody else needed to be moved, because they're all able-bodied." Eden said as she watched the big man gently set Suzanne down in one of the few chairs in one of the four sectioned-off rooms that all faced the vault.

She felt the buzz, just one. "We have one minute. Because they're blowing open the gate, we're not supposed to feel anything, but Asher said, just in case, we should take cover. This is the best cover I could think of for the Señora."

This time Leland didn't ask any questions. He just grabbed the arms of the chair that Suzanne was sitting in and leaned his body over hers. When the muffled pop came, it was negligible.

Yay, score one for the good guys.

"So, Eden, now explain to me why you're the point of contact. I'm eager to know." She grinned at his thinly veiled sarcasm.

"Well, Leland," she countered, using his given name for the first time. "Why don't you ask Suzanne?"

"Yes, why don't you?" the woman rasped up at him.

"I really don't care which one of you explains it to me, as long as you do it fast," he said switching to Spanish.

"Eden has confirmed with the Americans that the entire Nomad Security team is under a cloud of suspicion. Are they in bed with Maduro or not?"

He sighed. "Yeah, I haven't said much to either Patel or Carlson ever since their boss absconded to Aruba."

Suzanne pushed against the arms of the chair so she could sit up straighter and Leland helped her. She gave him a grateful, yet regal smile of thanks.

"Actually, it gets worse," Suzanne said. Then she started to cough.

"Let me talk. You rest your throat." Eden turned to Leland. "We now have reason to believe that Becker could possibly be working for Maduro as well. Right now, there is a computer expert with the SEALs who is trying to follow the money."

"Why in the hell didn't you tell me this? For God's sake Suzanne, I have forensic accountants coming out my ass. I could have been working on this since the moment you had suspicions."

The woman sat up straighter, her eyes blazing fire. "I own a bank. Like I don't." She shoved a finger at his chest as her voice came out in a choked whisper.

"Save your voice, Woman."

As interesting as the byplay was, Eden's breasts buzzed once, and that took her attention away from them.

"Gotta make a call. And I'll tell you what, Leland, I'll let you listen in."

"Mighty nice of you."

"Sarcasm doesn't become you," she said with a half-smile.

"Uh-huh, why don't you tell me something I care about?"

Suzanne let out a wheeze of laughter. Both Eden and Leland admonished her to be careful at the same time.

"I'm fine," the Señora assured them. "Make the call, Eden."

Eden turned away from Leland as she unbuttoned the top buttons of her cream silk blouse and fished out her phone from her underwire bra. She set the phone on the arm of Suzanne's chair and pressed in the number for Asher's phone.

"I'm inside the gate," Asher said instead of hello.

"What's next?" Eden asked.

"Four of us are going into the building through the back entrance. We've overridden the security codes, so we get in without key card passes."

"How?" Leland started to ask. "Never mind. You're getting in, that's the important thing. Then what?"

"Who's this?" Asher asked sharply.

"It's Leland Hines," Eden stepped in quickly. "We're down in the basement beside the vault with Señora Azua."

"That's all?"

"Yep. I figured this would be the safest place for someone who is injured."

"Agreed," Asher murmured. "We're going to be able to get all of you out through the opening that we've blown through the gate. Then we'll get everyone where they need to be. Let's start with Señora Azua since she's injured. It also helps that she is out of sight of Nomad Security and Heinrich Becker. We're going to have to figure out a way to get the rest of the people away from them."

"Let me work on that," Eden said. Possibilities were already beginning to roll through her mind. *Maybe they could be lured to the documents floor for some reason?*

"The back entrance is through the maintenance area. In order to not be seen, we're going to go around to the mezzanine, then the front staircase back down to the basement. Two of us will be there as quick as we can," Asher assured her.

"Okay," Eden answered, but she was talking to dead air.

"Eden," Suzanne grasped her hand.

"Yes?" She wanted to be respectful and listen, but she really wanted to see how she could possibly trap Becker, Patel, and Carlson in Suzanne's office.

"Take care of my employees first." The woman's voice sounded the strongest it had been in hours.

"Suzanne, we'll take care of you *and* your employees. Trust us," Leland answered.

Eden patted her hand as she picked up her phone and shoved it back into her bra. "I have an idea. If it works, we'll all be out of here with no problems. I've got to go."

As she started toward the door of the large office, Leland halted her. "What are you going to do?"

"Don't worry, I've got this," she assured him.

"I'll damn well worry if I want to," the man growled down at her. "What in the hell do you think you're going to accomplish that I couldn't do better?"

"I'm going to finesse some of the players into believing that they need to get together in the Señora's office for instructions from the Americans. Then, when I have them in there, I intend to figure out a way to lock them in."

Leland snorted. "Oh, really? How do you intend to do that? What else do you have tucked into your bra that I don't know about?"

Eden stood up to her full five-foot-nine inches and glared at the man. "Look here," she started.

"Ah, shit, I don't have time for this. I'll wait for the SEALs and tell them where you are. In the meantime, take this." He shoved a pistol into her hand. Eden gleefully gripped the Sig Sauer—it felt wonderful to have a gun in the palm of her hand. It was a little bigger than what she was used to, but damn, it packed a punch.

"You were always my favorite banker, Leland." She reached up and pecked him on the cheek then raced to the door to the stairs. Before she opened it, she ensured the safety was on, then untucked her blouse from the waistband of her skirt and shoved the gun underneath it.

All four SEALs looked over the thick balustrade of the mezzanine and viewed the baroque-decorated lobby of the bank. Overhead were four brass chandeliers and the floor was polished marble. Directly across from them was the teller area, which was still done in the old-fashioned mahogany wood and bronze bars—no bulletproof security glass for them. All windows were locked shut and the entire area behind the teller stations was unlit and looked to be locked off.

It seemed disconcerting to then have cubicles set up along the left and right walls instead of desks, but there they were. Along the left wall was the entrance to the women's restroom, along the right was the men's room.

"Do you see it?" Nic nudged Asher as he pointed to the exit sign to the left, next to the women's restroom.

"Are you asking him if he sees the obvious there? Li'l Nic?" Raiden drawled.

Nic flushed.

"We need to get into the teller area so we can be watching the entrance to the bank and see the offices on the left and right of the entrance," Ezio said.

Asher had been thinking the same thing. It gave him the heebie-jeebies not to be able to see the entry point of any building.

"I've got that covered. You have won the surveillance lottery. I want eyes and ears into Señora Azua's office."

He glanced over to the left-hand corner of the mezzanine level. They all knew that directly beneath that was Suzanne Azua's office. But this bank had been built back in the day when real artisans and builders had been hired, so the floors were thick and solid. How in the hell he was going to get through the floor to surveil the people was anybody's guess.

"Thanks a lot." Ezio smiled as he backtracked away from the balustrade and went toward the dark corner.

Asher liked the fact that Ezio hadn't been flipping him shit when he'd thanked him for the assignment. Instead, he was gleeful. He was looking forward to figuring out a way to do the impossible. He might just be a good asset to Night Storm after all.

"What fun do you want to give us?" Raiden asked.

Asher looked into his friend's calm dark eyes. That was Raiden—always someone he could count on to be your eye in the middle of a storm.

"I want the main elevators out of commission. According to Eden, everybody but the three of them are on the lobby level, but that could change on a dime. Get those elevators shut down."

"Nic, you're with me," Raiden said. Asher watched as the two of them melted into the shadows.

Asher knew they were headed to the sub-basement. Now he had to make contact with Eden as well as secure the teller area. He could take out both of those priorities at the same time, since there was a secure staircase and an elevator that went between the lobby teller area and the vault area in the basement. It totally bypassed the document room below the lobby floor. So, he just needed to get to the basement.

Asher pushed away from the balustrade to head to the East staircase when he caught movement out of the corner of his eye. The long black ponytail swished as the woman quietly shut the west staircase door shut on the lobby floor next to the women's restroom. He zeroed in on her face. He recognized her from the files that Kane had provided.

It was Eden York.

Goddammit, why isn't she still in the basement?

CHAPTER 8

Dammit!

Her boobs just buzzed twice.

Doesn't Asher know I have a plan? I don't have time to call his ass back.

Eden was really itching to use the gun. Not that she was going to, that would just be stupid. Didn't mean she didn't *want* to.

Fine.

She looked around the lobby. No sign of the bank employees. She saw Marco talking to one of the other bank guards. She gave him a head nod, then he turned back to the guard. *Good.* She darted back to the stairwell.

She pressed in the number to Asher's satellite phone as soon as the door closed behind her. It took three rings before he picked up.

What the hell? He was the one who wanted me to call back so damned fast.

"Stay where you are" were the first words out of his mouth.

It took her a moment. "Did you see me in the lobby? Where were you? I thought you were outside the bank. You got in? That was fast."

"Geez, Lady, one question at a time. First, getting in fast is what we do. Second, you were supposed to be in the basement. Now, get back there." She recognized that tone of voice. He sounded like every other typical overbearing male in her life. Well, he wasn't her father or one of her older brothers. And it wasn't like she took orders from the men in her family anyway.

"No way, Asher. I have a plan." She hit the bar on the door so she could go back to the lobby.

"Don't you dare." The hair on the back of her neck stood up. She could almost feel the warm air of his voice as he rumbled into the phone.

Eden hesitated. Should she listen? Dammit, they needed a diversion. His team was probably all kitted out in little camo uniforms—they couldn't divert Carlson, Patel, and Becker, but she could. She started to push the door open.

A big hand covered hers and yanked the door shut. "What the hell did you not understand about stay still?" Asher growled into her ear.

Eden shivered.

She turned slowly around and looked up to see blue eyes blazing down at her. There was nothing typical about this male. He was the antithesis of typical, but...

Oh.

My.
God.
He was *male*.

"I have a plan." Was that squeaky voice hers?

"So, do I. It includes you getting your tushie down to the vault with the others and letting me and my men rescue the bankers and getting them safely on a plane," he snapped down at her.

Eden sighed. They were back to *typical*.

"Nice to meet you too, Asher."

"It would have been nicer to meet you if you'd been in the basement, Eden." His sarcasm was hard to miss.

"Well, if wishes were horses, beggars would ride."

His lip twitched.

"Humor isn't getting you downstairs any faster. Seriously, I need you to move your ass, so we can get our job done."

She pointed her finger and twirled it up and down the front of his body. "So, tell me, Army boy, in all your fatigue finery, how are you planning on blending in and culling the herd without Patel, Carlson, and Becker taking notice?"

"We've got it covered, but you running around fucking things up with some cockamamie plan is not going to help things."

"Really, that's how they're training special forces these days? Turning down help? Rigidly staying to plan instead adapting to changing circumstances."

Asher's eyes narrowed. "Interesting phraseology," he

drawled slowly, his eyes clearly assessing her in a different light.

Gotcha!

"You said there were only seven men. Seems to me that having Leland and me as extra hands would be a Godsend."

He took a deep breath. "Okay, Ms. York, lay it on me."

"Well, it's a partial plan. It totally depends on who's in the office. When I left, Carlson was in the office, and I passed Patel heading into the there too, as I took Suzanne to the stairway. Hell, I don't know if they're still there or not. God knows who's where. But I thought I would gather them up in the office. Hopefully track down Becker while I was at it. I figured I could tell them that Suzanne had died, and that the real reason Maduro's men wanted into the bank was the gold in the vault or some such shit."

His eyes widened. It was that same incredulous look she'd seen on her dad's face far too many times.

"We're getting your tushie down to the basement." His voice brooked no argument.

"But—"

"It's a half-baked plan and you know it."

She grabbed Asher's arm. "You don't understand, the best part of the plan is the 'some such shit.' I'm really good at flying by the seat of my pants. I really will figure something out. It'll be good, and I'll get those men into the office and hold them there."

She whipped out the gun from the back of her skirt and held it up in front of his face to show him.

"Jesus. Put that away. What the fuck, Eden? Where did you get that?"

"Leland gave it to me. Trust me, I know how to use it. Don't be a pussy, the safety's on."

He was going to kill Kane. Why in the hell did they not have a file on this woman? He was flying blind with just her resume and hot-looking picture. There was a hell of a lot more under the surface, and he hated not knowing what he was dealing with. But there was definitely something more than just a translator, and it was time for Kane to start digging.

"Put the gun away, Eden. You're right, we could use another set of hands. How well can you shoot?"

"My brother Pete is one of the owners of Force-Tactical out of Vegas. He's taught me a few things."

Ah-ha. That explained a lot right there. Pete York was an amputee who had taken early retirement from the Green Berets and started a firearms, martial arts and combat training center run entirely by disabled vets. If Eden had been trained by her brother, she was good as gold.

"I still need you to get—" he started as patiently as he could.

"My tushie down to the basement. Yeah, yeah, I heard you the first few times."

She was giving in, he could hear it in her voice. It was time to press his advantage.

"Look, Eden, I like the idea of brainstorming, but let's not do the fly-by-the-seat-of-our-pants part. You don't know what the rest of my team has planned. You don't know if all three of those guys are bad guys. There are too many variables."

Intelligent green eyes twinkled up at him. "But look, gun." She held up the pistol again and grinned when he winced.

"And it's called a some-such-shit plan. It'll work," she cajoled.

"You are so trying to play me. It's not going to work. Did it ever work with Pete?"

"Sure, when I was five or ten. However, it stopped working with my dad and brothers as soon as I was dating age. Downstairs, right?"

"Damn right. I want you where I can see you."

"Fine," she huffed. "But if you don't have a good plan, I'm going for it. Remember. Gun." She went to reach for it again.

He held up his hands. "Stop already. Remember. SEAL."

She rolled her eyes and started down the stairs two at a time. That was in a pencil skirt that showed off a very nice ass. Before she could reach for the handle of the basement door, he stopped her.

"Now what?"

"We proceed with caution."

"Maduro's men are outside," she started to protest.

Then she gasped. "Damn, you're right. I'm an idiot." She pulled the damn gun from the small of her back. Holy hell, she was a hundred times worse than Cullen's sisters. He was so screwed.

"Me first," he demanded.

"Agreed." *At last, a little bit of sense.* He raised his eyebrow in a question.

"You have body armor. But I have your back," she assured him.

He quietly opened the door. The lights were dim.

"The lights were always low," she answered his unasked question. "The lights are on in the back office where Leland and Suzanne are." Her voice was barely a whisper.

He made his way across the hall, between the offices and what he assumed was the walled-off vault. He didn't hear a sound behind him. He turned and saw that Eden was holding her shoes and walking in her stocking-covered feet.

Asher heard a man talking.

"I told you not to talk. Just write down what you want to tell me." The man was clearly agitated.

Asher relaxed. That had to be Leland talking to Suzanne Azua. Still, he wasn't taking any chances. He checked every office on his way down the hall, ensuring they were empty. Eden kept her post at each of the doors, covering him. Yep, she had definitely trained with her brother.

"No, I'm not sure what Eden is going to do, but I trust her instincts," Leland was saying.

Eden sauntered into the office in front of Asher. "Thanks for the vote of confidence, Leland. I appreciate it."

Leland did a double-take when he saw Asher following her into the office.

"I have to admit, I'm pretty damn glad to see you with our girl," Leland grinned at Asher. "She was hellbent on doing something to help, but I like the idea of her being somewhere safe better."

"Me too," Suzanne rasped.

"Oh, one way or another, I'm going to help. This is just a pitstop while Asher explains his plan. Or should I say, as he develops his plan."

Asher went over to the woman who was trying to sit up in the chair. Even with the blue blood-stained scarf wrapped around her neck, she looked regal. He could see where Cynthia got her good looks. *Let's just hope she's as feisty as Lenora.*

He crouched down in front of her. "It's good to meet you, Señora. I am very impressed with your family. They are worried about you, and I promised that I would be bringing you home soon."

Suzanne smiled. "I'm proud of them," Suzanne said before she started to cough.

"Write it down, Woman." Leland glowered at her.

Suzanne closed her eyes. If Asher had to guess, she was praying for patience. She took the proffered notepad from Leland and started to write.

Asher read her note aloud.

I hate the thought that my actions on this council might have put any of my family in danger.

"Seems to me that your nephew courts danger," Asher teased gently.

Suzanne sighed her agreement.

"Asher, are you in charge of this op?" Eden asked.

"I'm taking point on-site. My lieutenant and the second-in-command are outside determining the best way to ensure that Maduro's men don't infiltrate the bank. Ultimately, we want to get you out with no casualties."

"Good thinking," Leland clapped Asher on the back. "Keep all non-combatants alive, that should always be the mandate. Do you have any idea why they haven't just led an all-out assault? If Maduro is out to get us, we're sitting ducks. Now's the time."

"Maduro is busy being entertained on the Isla de Margarita. He's incommunicado. According to our sources, he won't be back until Sunday morning to attend Mass, so we're safe until then."

Suzanne shook her head, then winced as she gingerly touched her throat. She then demanded her notepad back from Asher with an imperious wave of her hand. He handed it to her.

Untrue, Perez is his right-hand man. Maduro's secret police will listen to him. Perez is greedy. Might make move on the bank without Maduro.

"Yeah, but that would piss off Maduro," Asher said with a frown.

Suzanne underlined the words greedy and bank.

The light dawned.

"Fuck me. He couldn't care less about your cash, it's worthless. Hell, in order to buy a loaf of bread, people are weighing the cash instead of counting it out. But you have gold stashed away here in the bank, don't you?" How could he, Kane, and Max have missed this?

She nodded, then wrote again.

Safety deposit boxes.

"How much total?" Asher asked.

For the first time, Suzanne's eyes cut away from his.

"Never mind, you don't have to tell me your bank's assets. It's enough to know that it could encourage the cockroaches." Asher's head felt like it was going to explode; he didn't know if it was from the crash or because they'd screwed the pooch so badly.

"I've got to get my team on the phone," Asher said as he pulled his satellite phone out of his tactical vest. "I need to get some background on Perez and find out if he's one of the bastards who currently have us surrounded."

He started out of the room and caught Eden's grin. "Yeah, yeah, I remember," he smiled reluctantly.

"*Now* you don't think my plan was all that farfetched, do you? It's all about the creative thinking, SEAL boy."

She was beautiful. She was smart. And she scared the hell out of him.

He watched as Suzanne motioned for Leland and Eden to come closer. It looked like something important. But he didn't have time to go and see what the hell was going on, he needed to talk to his team.

Asher moved to the office furthest away from the Eden and the others and tagged Kane.

"What?" Kane's voice was gruff as he answered the phone.

"You okay?" Asher asked.

"There's a lot of variables. It's about goddamn time you called in. I've heard from Raiden and Ezio. So, what have you got for me?"

"More than either of us want," Asher said as he leaned against the wall and kept his eye on the door to the staircase and the office down the hall. "We have a bank full of gold and safety deposit boxes that one of Maduro's men, a guy named Perez, is itching to get his hands on."

"Perez?" Kane asked. "If you give me a minute or two, I'll pull him up."

"While you're at it, I want the full fucking run-down on Eden York. Did you know that her brother is Pete York, the former Green Beret who operates Force-Tactical out of Vegas?"

"No shit. I've met him."

Asher could hear the grin in Kane's voice.

"Well, I've now met his sister, and she's a wildcard. She intends to be part of this op, and the only thing that is going to stop her is locking her in the bank vault."

"Dammit, Thorne, that's the last thing we need, some damned civilian thinking they can help us out. She'll get herself killed and fuck up the mission. You've got to sit on her!"

Asher sighed. "Kane, the crap thing is? I think she could be of help."

"You're shitting me."

"Get me the file on her. I want it the same time you find out about Perez. When I ran into her twenty minutes ago, she had a Sig Sauer in her hand and had a harebrained plan that ended up being pretty damned good. Since I don't know where we stand with Becker, Patel, and Carlson, I think having her around to help sort shit out will help."

"Think this through, she's a fucking civilian!"

"Do you think I don't know that?" Asher kept his voice down, barely. "Just do what I tell you to do. You're the one with the info, so get it to me. There is more to this woman than being an interpreter, and I want to know what it is. Hell, I think she might have been a Girl Scout."

Kane barked out a laugh. "Nah, she was probably just a Camp Fire Girl."

"Get me the info."

CHAPTER 9

As soon as Asher came back into the office, Eden knew that she had won. She was going to get to help. Officially. Not that she wouldn't have done what she would've wanted to do anyway, it was just easier to be on the payroll officially, so to speak.

"What's the plan?" Leland asked before she had a chance to.

"Well, I'll tell you what's happening right now." Asher pulled out the chair from behind the office desk for Eden to sit down. She gave him a jaunty smile and sat. It was easy to smile and be happy now that she knew she was getting her way.

She totally felt vindicated. It meant that Asher must have gone to bat for her. They'd only really met twenty minutes ago, but he'd found value in her in just that amount of time. That tugged at her. Made her feel really good. Yeah, in her job as a translator she was well-respected, but to have someone like Asher Thorne really see her value in a situation like this made her feel worthy in his estimation. And that was important to her.

Her mouth quivered into a smile as she stopped with the mushy stuff. What was really important was that the man was positively delicious. Now *that* was a real reason to smile.

Focus, York.

Surrounded by bad guys, remember?

Still. Those blue eyes.

She sat down and he leaned against the desk so he could look over all of them. "I have three other men here in the bank building with me. Two of them are working on disabling the elevators. One is working to get eyes and ears on your office, Señora."

They all nodded. Made sense so far.

"On the outside coordinating our effort is my lieutenant and the second-in-command who is our computer genius. He's pulling up everything he can on Perez to see if there are any weak spots we can exploit. Then there's our resident wildcard who was out front working with your nephew," Asher said as he nodded to Suzanne.

Asher had been reluctant to mention that bit of information, but knew he needed to be as transparent as possible.

"What has Rafa got to do with all of this?" Suzanne asked in a calm whisper.

"While we were blowing our way into the back gate, we needed a diversion. He and Cullen used the food truck to give away free food to keep all of the civilians away from the blast site."

"If you say one more word, instead of writing it down, Suzanne, there will be holy hell to pay," Leland said as he leaned over her. The woman was not intimidated.

Asher almost laughed at the byplay and would have if they weren't in such deep shit. He noticed Eden's eyes twinkling. He did laugh when she winked at him.

"What is so damned funny?" Leland demanded to know. "Eden, check her throat. Make sure it isn't swelling worse than it was because she's talking so much."

Suzanne's pen dug into the notepad as she quickly wrote something down and handed it to Leland.

"What did she say?" Eden asked.

"Nothing worth repeating," Leland said as he glared at Suzanne. "Please check her out."

Asher watched as Eden competently examined the woman's neck and throat. "Damn. Suzanne, you should have raised your hand. Why didn't you tell me you were in pain?" Eden looked up at Asher with an intense expression on her face. "We need ice. I need to go upstairs."

"Send Leland," Ash said.

"What's wrong? How bad is it?" He cupped Suzanne's shoulder and leaned in. "Woman, why didn't I notice that the swelling had gotten worse?"

"Because, scarf," Suzanne croaked out the two words.

"I'll be right back with ice." Leland stood up straight.

"Bullshit," Eden said. "Everybody is expecting me to be the one to get the ice for Suzanne. I've been doing it since we arrived. If Leland starts doing it then there are bound to be questions."

"Nobody but the clerical workers will notice," Leland protested. "Eden, we don't have time to argue."

"This is important, Leland. The bank guards will notice you're getting the ice. Don't think they won't. That'll be a red flag. They'll approach you, start asking questions, and eventually be down here." Her hand sliced through the air. "Conversation closed. I'm going."

Asher snorted. "Seriously, is this how you did your job as an interpreter? I'm surprised anyone hired you. You need to learn when to take an order."

"Not the same thing. This is a fluid life-and-death situation. We need everybody cooperating to stay alive. Now, if you have something better than me getting the ice—and fast—let 'er rip. But the Leland idea is crap."

All that fire. God, she was compelling. She was wrong, but damned hot.

"You're wrong. What we want is one of the guards, that guy named Torres, to notice Leland and come on down. This would be a perfect way to get him in on what's going on without our suspects suspecting anything."

Eden opened her mouth to disagree. He could tell it was a knee-jerk reaction, but she shut it, instead nodded her head. "You're right."

Asher's radio clicked. He picked up. "Yeah?"

"I've got eyes and ears," Ezio said.

He was liking this Omega Sky guy more and more. "Give me the status."

"Five people. Four men, and one woman. Speaking English. I recognize Carlson's voice. One has been referred to as Heinrich. The woman is a tall blonde. One man is overweight, and the other man is Asian. That's all I've got," he said apologetically.

"Our only wildcard is Patel," Leland said. "I'm going. I've got my phone. I'll call Eden if I have any problems."

Asher nodded in agreement.

"Good luck," Eden encouraged as Leland strode out the door. She bent and checked Suzanne another time, even though the woman tried to wave her away.

"You'll be doing good once we get some ice on you again." Then she stood up and looked at Asher. "Is that thing on?" she nodded to the radio.

Ash nodded.

"The people you saw are Heinrich Becker, he's the IMF Chairman, you know Carlson, the tall blond woman is Dr. Gerta Nilsson. Gerta may or may not be in cahoots with Becker." She looked up at Asher. "Your computer genius is following Becker's money to see if he has anything going on with Maduro, right?"

Ash nodded at Eden. He was less than happy, because his friend the guru was late.

"So, who else?" Ezio's voice came through the radio.

"Kaito Nakamura is the Japanese man. He's our international stock market expert."

"Do you speak Japanese?" Asher asked.

"Some. But Kaito's fluent in English."

"Ezio, we've got Eden York, Leland Hines, and Suzanne Azua here in the basement. At least we did. Leland just left to get ice for the Señora's neck wound. Let us know the second anyone leaves the office."

"Roger that."

Asher clicked on his radio. "Raiden. What's the status with the elevators?"

"Give me two more minutes, and they'll be disabled. No explosives necessary."

"How in the hell did you manage that?" Asher demanded.

"These are an old brand with a specific hoist motor and pendant controller. Nic was able to YouTube how to cripple it. It'll take new parts to fix." He could hear the pride in Raiden's voice.

Gotta love you some YouTube.

Eden heard Asher's radio click again. It was the first guy, the one who had eyes and ears on Suzanne's office.

"Another guy just joined the party. He's American. He's holding a bag of ice. He and Carlson are yelling at one another."

Fuckity fuck fuck. I'm not going to scream.

What is Leland doing in there? He needs to be coming down here with ice for Suzanne.

Suzanne started to cough. Asher had moved to the

door of the office when Leland had left so that he could monitor the stairs. He rushed back to Suzanne's side when she started to cough.

He hit the button on his radio. "You done with that elevator, Raiden?" His voice was clipped.

"One more minute. What's up?"

"Need a medic down here. Stat."

"Nic, finish up," Eden heard the man say. "Asher, I'll be down to the basement in less than a minute. I've got my med kit."

Thank God.

Eden looked down at her hand and was amazed it wasn't trembling. She'd talked a good game to Kane, but the idea of having to perform a tracheotomy on Suzanne Azua scared the shit out of her.

"I'm going to direct Raiden this way," Asher said before he ran out of the office.

Suzanne wheezed.

"Help will be right here." Eden grabbed the one bottle of water they had and cleaned off as much blood as she could from where she judged Suzanne's windpipe to be. Suzanne whimpered and Eden wanted to cry.

She gripped Suzanne's hand and looked her dead in the eye. "It's going to be okay. These guys are supermen. Don't pay any attention to all the shit I've been giving them, they will save your life, do your dry cleaning, and then cook your dinner. You'll see."

She saw Suzanne's eyes sparkle before her face suffused with pain.

Fucking hurry!

A door slammed.

Almost before she could turn around, a big, rough-looking man was skidding on his knees beside Eden, knife, and tubing in his hand.

"Good job on wiping the area clean," he said as he grappled with his utility pouch. He yanked it off his tactical vest and shoved it at her. "Grab the antiseptic wipes."

"Asher, down here. Help me get her on the floor."

"You got it Raiden," Asher answered.

As soon as Suzanne was lying prone, he cupped her cheek. He put his ear next to her mouth and grimaced.

"Gotta do this now."

Eden handed him the moist towelette.

"Have gauze ready," he commanded. Then he cleansed the area and wiped off the knife. He wasted no time in making a deep cut in her neck. As soon as he pierced her windpipe, Suzanne's chest heaved upwards as she took in a deep breath. Raiden was inserting the surgical tubing as Eden tried to work around him and stop the flow of blood around the cut.

"Slower," Eden told Suzanne as she brushed back her hair. "You have air now, don't take tiny breaths, nice even breathing," she advised. Out of the corner of her eye, she watched as Raiden applied tape to the surgical tubing to keep it in place.

"What now?" she asked Asher.

"Now, we get her to a hospital, just like we said in the beginning." His smile was calm and soothing.

"Just going to walk on out the front door and put her in an ambulance, are you?"

He turned to Raiden, "Sarcasm is how she deals with stress," he explained.

"Answer the damned question."

Asher came closer and put his hand on her shoulder and squeezed. Eden was surprised at the amount of comfort she took in the act, especially since he hadn't proven himself to her yet. *But hasn't he?* Hadn't she finally met somebody cut of the same cloth as the men in her family? At last?

There was something about Asher Thorne that made her want to lean on him. Something about him that made her ache to believe in him. She shrugged it off; she needed to focus on the fact that they were still stuck in the bank, and Suzanne still needed to get to a hospital.

"We're going to get Señora Azua out the same way we came in. My lieutenant will be waiting to take her to the hospital on the other side of the gate. You'll see, she'll be in a private room with her mother and daughter real soon."

Her heart clenched at his steady words.

"I want to believe you," she whispered.

"You can," he whispered back. "You can, Eden."

He crouched down and lifted Suzanne up as gently as Leland had, then his radio crackled. "Ash, we've got a problem."

Eden didn't recognize the voice.

Raiden finished stuffing supplies back into his utility

pouch and stood up. He made a motion and Asher shifted Suzanne into his arms. Raiden spoke into his microphone. "Nic, get down to the basement, now!"

"What's the problem, Cullen?" Asher asked.

"There's a tank that's coming down the boulevard. Right now, everyone is ignoring it, thinking it is part of the parade, but it's not. It's coming straight to the bank."

A tank?

Eden heard the door to the stairway open again, she put her head out and saw a young blonde man in uniform. It had to be Nic. "This way," she motioned.

Raiden brushed past her holding Suzanne. "You're blocking for me, Nic. We're taking her through the gate. Need to get her to a hospital. Asher, tell—"

"I'm on it," Asher said as he waved Raiden away.

"Cullen, Raiden just trached Señora Azua. He and Nic will be coming out with her. She needs transport to a hospital. You got it?"

Eden heard Cullen say, "Rafa."

"I don't care if it's a fucking water taxi, just get 'er done. I asked Kane for files on some people thirty minutes ago. What's his problem?"

"Ash, this is Kane. I've been monitoring all the chatter. Been waiting for you to have a moment to go offline so I could give you the debrief, or did you want me to cut in and debrief you now?" His tone was sarcastic.

She saw Asher wince.

"Roger that." Was Asher's response.

"Ash, this is Leo." That was a new name. "Rafa's in

position to pick up his aunt. The hospital has been notified. We also have eyes on the tank. It's an Alvis Scorpion."

"Oh shit. Are you sure?"

Asher seemed really worried. This was not good.

"Yep. One of Rafa's friends posted it on their Instagram."

"Did you say Instagram?" Asher asked.

"Can it, Thorne," Kane grumbled. "We've got to get everybody the hell out of there, now."

Asher turned to Eden. "What's your gut telling you? Who's the bad guy? Becker or Carlson?"

Eden grimaced and ran her fingers through her tangled hair, then gave up. "Carlson's an asshole, no doubt. He got us the hell out of dodge when we were in trouble though; why would he do that if he wanted to serve us up to Maduro?"

"On the other hand, Becker's reputation with the IMF is pristine, the work he's done for different countries has been unbelievable. I thought he came from money, so I don't know why he would be trying to siphon off more."

"Okay, you told me what your head is telling you. What's your gut saying?" Asher was looking at her encouragingly. It was clear he really wanted to know what she thought.

"They're both dirty as fuck. I don't know why. But as soon as I saw that note from Suzanne, it clicked. Gerta's not in on it, and it's scaring the hell out of me that Leland's up in that office with them. Not so much

Becker, he won't get his hands dirty, but Carlson? He'll kill him."

Asher nodded.

"You got that, Kane?"

"Got it."

"What have you managed to find out?" Asher asked.

"Nomad Security is as clean as everybody in the industry thought."

Eden opened her mouth to protest, and Asher held up his hand.

"But," Kane continued. "Now that we did a deeper check, it turns out that Phil Carlson retired in New Mexico seven years ago. Supposedly, he came out of retirement for this gig, but it wasn't him. Phil's still in New Mexico and this guy, whoever the hell he is, has taken his place. He could be working with Becker, he could be a plant for Maduro, or he could be freelance. Don't know yet. But Eden, your gut was right."

"And Becker?" she asked.

"He comes from old, old, old money. The kind that's been helped along by profiteering on every single war since the Dutch War of Independence, and right now his nephew is being investigated for having ties to the blood diamond trade."

Eden looked at Ash. They were in perfect accord.

"The bastard. The absolute bastard. He's using his knowledge on the IMF to figure out how to line his pockets."

I am not going to cry. And if I am, it's because I'm angry, not because I'm disillusioned.

"Get the fuck out of there," Kane told Asher.

"I'm going to get Eden out. Then I'll work on getting the rest out."

"Bad plan. I'm staying."

"Going black for a minute," Asher said.

"Don't—" Kane was shut off before he could finish.

CHAPTER 10

The sheen of tears in Eden's eyes had damn near gutted him.

"Eden?"

"I'm staying," she said fiercely. "You need my help."

"Talk to me. We have thirty seconds, then you can be Wonder Woman, I promise."

He couldn't help himself, his fingers brushed at the soft, delicate skin of her tearstained cheek. "Just tell me, Baby."

"People are starving, dying, being butchered. He was supposed to be their savior, but he's profiting? He's trying to make these conflicts last longer so he can make money?" There was such anguish in her green eyes.

Her hand whipped up and grabbed his. Her grip was strong. "Promise me we'll get him. We'll make him pay. Promise me we won't ever let him do this again."

Asher grinned slowly. She was like a diamond, so many facets that glittered brilliantly, they tantalized the imagination. Here he was in the middle of one of the worst ops of his life, because so many civilians were depending on them, and he'd found an extraordinary woman. How was that possible? Was he just reeling from Xavier's death and looking for some kind of unique closeness to fill the void left by his big brother? Or was it something like what Kane and Cullen had found with their women?

"Do you promise, Asher? Do you promise me?" Her voice trembled.

He brought their clasped hands up to her cheek and pulled out his index finger so he could trace her trembling lower lip.

"It would take a man forever to figure you out, wouldn't it?"

"What?" she blinked up at him. Confused.

"I promise, he's going down."

She gave a relieved smile. "Thank you."

"You didn't have to ask, Honey."

Eden blinked slowly and then her eyes were dry. "Turn on your radio, I'm done with my meltdown. We've got civilians to rescue and bad guys to catch."

Asher flipped the switch on his mic.

"Asher, you do that again, and it goes in your file." Max was pissed off. "You got me?"

"Yes, sir."

"Suzanne is on the way with Rafa to the hospital. Raiden, Cullen, and Nic are at the opening, coming back in. The plan is back in place, Ezio is hitting the lights in two minutes. He's going to rappel over the side of the balustrade to take the people in Señora Azua's office by surprise. When the rest of the team comes through the blast hole, they'll clear out the people on the lobby floor—that includes guards and civilians. You'll join them."

"I can help gather everybody," Eden chimed in.

Asher and Max said 'No' simultaneously.

"Yes," she ground out. She stood up from where she'd been slumped against the side of the desk. "How many stupid-ass rescue operations go FUBAR because some civilian panics and doesn't do what they're told? I'm thinking a whole hell of a lot. The people know me, plus I'm a woman, I can help. Trust me, you don't know Sharon Foster, she has a hissy fit if she gets a run in her hose. The lights going out are going to send her into orbit."

"I said no, Eden." Asher was proud of how calm his voice was.

He watched her give him a considering look and sigh. "Fine, but if things start falling to shit, and you find out you need me with a screamy-meemy-Sharon, are you going to ask for my help?"

Asher looked up at the ceiling, then down at her determined green eyes. "I promise to adapt to changing circumstances."

She grinned at him.

"That's all I can ask for."

He pulled a small flashlight out of his pack and wrapped his arm around her waist. "Let's go."

∽

They were in the stairway when the lights went out and the red emergency light came on. It was dim, but Asher wasn't surprised in the least that Eden was surefooted, even in her little kitten heels. He hadn't even needed to tell her to put them back on, she'd known to do it as soon as he'd explained they were going to go through a hole in the gate that he'd blown through.

"My team will be coming through the gate at the northeast. They'll let themselves in through the maintenance door at the east wall lobby, near the elevators."

Asher continued. "Our headcount is seventeen. Ten civilians, counting you. Two Nomad Security, five bank guards, one of which is Torres. Ezio's up on the mezzanine; he's going to keep eyes on the people in the office and also pinpoint the whereabouts of the others on the lobby floor. That will allow Cullen, Raiden, and Nic to gather them up and take them to safety."

"I wanna believe, please know I want to believe," she whispered. "But I'm a cynical bitch who always plans for the worst."

"Planning for the worst is what we do too. That's the reason I'm not taking you directly to safety, just in case you're right and we *do* need you. But I sure as hell am hoping for the best."

He quietly opened the door to the lobby near the women's restroom and ushered her through it.

She was silent as a mouse. He looked down. She'd taken off her shoes again. *Yep, her brother trained her well.*

"What happened?!" a woman was screaming in English. "Are they going to kill us?"

Asher kept his flashlight on, night vision goggles wouldn't work since light was still coming through the windows. "To the left, we're avoiding Suzanne's office." He whispered the words directly into her ear. She nodded.

"Be quiet," another woman said in Spanish. The situation was going to hell, fast.

"What are you saying?" the woman screamed back at her in English. She had a British accent.

"I take it that's Sharon?" Asher whispered.

Eden nodded.

"You need to calm down, Señorita." A man entered the fray. Sharon continued to shout. Obviously, his soothing was having no effect, as she continued to yell in fear.

Asher pinpointed where the conversation was coming from—one of the cubicles near the men's restrooms. "Ezio, do you have eyes on this?" he asked into his mic.

"Yeah, they closed the office door as soon as the lights went out. I'm looking over the balustrade and I've got eyes on the screamer. She's surrounded by a suit, a guard, and another woman."

"Ezio, how many in the office?" Asher demanded to know.

"It's changed since my last report. Still the doughboy, then there's Heinrich, Carlson and Kaito. The woman and Leland left as soon as the lights went out and the screaming started. The muffin man is squeezed himself under the desk, babbling in French, I think."

"That's Schlessinger. We're going to need a crane and an éclair to get him the hell out from under there," Eden said disgustedly.

"French?"

"Swiss, but he really only speaks French. I think I can talk him out from under the desk, and I can help with Sharon."

"Ezio can get Sharon, I already saw him in action with Rafa's girlfriends at the food truck. He's a natural. She'll be putty in his hands."

"Okay."

"We've got a problem," Max said urgently. "Big. The jeeps are moving out to make way for the tank. Get those civilians the hell out of there, *now!*" Asher knew that everyone on the transmission got the message.

"Ezio, you heard your job," Asher told his teammate.

"Yep, go charm the screamer. Easy, I've got this. That means I'll be scooping up at least four civilians. Probably a guard or two by then."

"Eden and I are going to the office. That will give us four."

"That leaves us eight who are scattered," Raiden said. "If we get them, then we'll come help you and Eden."

"Negative," Asher answered. "There will be three of us—Leland will be a calm head helping us. You go to Ezio first."

There was a pause. "Agreed," Cullen and Raiden said at the same time.

Because of the slippery lobby floor, Eden fell on her ass when the first blast hit. She scrambled to get up, but Asher covered her body.

"Stay down," he hissed.

She stilled. Another concussion hit, followed by crashing sounds and shattering glass, but Asher's body kept her from moving.

"So now I know what a tank hit feels like," she tried to tease. But truly she was beginning to get scared. She hated scared. Mad. Pissed. Angry. Those were acceptable feelings. Not scared. Being scared was for pussies.

She shoved at Asher's shoulders, the part of him that wasn't covered with Kevlar. The part that was all muscle. *Okay, feeling lustful.* That was one of the good feelings too.

"Let me up," she demanded.

"They're not done."

"Well, we have to hurry then," she growled up at him. Because of the dim light, she couldn't see his eyes, but she saw his jaw tense as his teeth probably ground together. She had that effect on men.

"You're just going to slide on your ass again. We wait."

Another blast, this time much worse, and she felt hot, humid air hit her. *Oh, holy hell.* They'd blasted through the bank wall. It sounded like the entire building was shrieking in pain as parts of it collapsed.

Sharon's shrieking had stopped between the second

and third blast. Eden prayed it was because Ezio had gotten her to safety.

"Oh hell no." Even through the cacophony of sound, Ezio's anguished words got through to Eden. She prayed to God that he was all right. That Sharon was all right.

Asher got up and found her shoes. "Put these on."

She did, and then he hauled her to her feet.

She looked around. Holy mother of God, there was a hole the size of a truck where the highly polished bronze doors of the entrance used to be.

"Quit staring, the tank is going to start rolling in. We've got to get to the office to show them the way out of here," Asher hollered. He had to yell because there was cement, wood, and stone crashing down around the hole and the sound was tremendous.

Now that the moonlight was shining in, Eden could see better. She saw Asher whip off his night-vision goggles as she ran toward Suzanne's office. Eden was not surprised to see men coming out. Leland was looking around, and when he spotted Asher and Eden, he grabbed at Carlson and Becker, but was only able to stop Carlson.

"Mike, go with him," Leland said, pointing at Asher. "He can lead you to safety."

Carlson ripped out of his grip.

"Fuck you, Hines," Carlson said before he took off across the lobby toward the teller cages.

What the hell?

"Leland," Asher yelled over the crumbling building. It was as if an earthquake had hit. Two of the gigantic light fixtures crashed down in the center of the lobby, glass shooting out everywhere. There was more screaming and yelling.

Eden heard people hollering in Spanish and English, trying to relay instructions. *Please God, say people will get to safety.*

She needed to focus—she might not like the man, but she needed to get to Maurice Schlessinger. Eden continued to run the rest of the way to the office, Asher at her side. The door was hanging off its hinges.

"Let me go first. It's not stable," Asher said. Both of the windows were blown out. The bookcase had been torn from the wall and was teetering on top of one of the leather chairs. But the desk was solid.

"Maurice," Eden called out. "Come out from under the desk. We can get you to safety."

Nothing.

"Maurice," she called louder.

Asher crouched down to look under the desk. "He's dead."

"But the desk should have protected him," Eden protested. She tried to shove past Asher so she could see for herself, but he blocked her. That didn't stop her from seeing an ever-widening pool of blood.

"What happened?" she asked in horror.

"A piece of glass got him in the jugular. He didn't have a chance." Asher stood up. "Come on, we've got to go."

Eden looked down at her shoes. They were bloody. She couldn't help taking a quick step backwards.

Dammit. Maurice didn't deserve this. Nobody deserved this.

Eden clamped her teeth together hard, so she wouldn't whimper.

Asher grabbed her hand. "We need to get out of here. Now."

She finally noticed that more dust was falling down on them, and that there was a loud rumbling that was getting noticeably louder. "What's that?"

"The tank, it's coming in."

Eden found herself rooted to the floor, looking down at the blood on her shoes. Asher grabbed her arm and hauled her out of the office. It was just what she needed to kick-start her into gear.

"Status," he yelled into his mic.

She heard the answer as it came through on Asher's radio's speaker.

"They've found eight. They're slotting them out of the northeast hole right now."

"Who's missing?" Eden questioned.

"Gerta, Becker and Carlson, they don't know who the other four are. They'll take a headcount when they're on the other side of the gate."

Eden did a quick headcount in her mind. Schlessinger would be one of the four.

"We've got to find the other three."

"If we find them on the way to getting you safe, then fine," Asher said as he looked to his right toward the stairs near the elevator. It was one of the exit points. It had taken a direct hit from one of the tank shells. That was out.

"There's only one other exit from the building," Asher yelled. "We need to move." He changed from gripping her to putting his arm around her waist. As soon as her wet shoe hit the highly polished floor, she understood why. Once again, she would have ended up on her ass.

The rumble was no longer a rumble, it was a roar. She looked behind her and saw the tank cross the threshold into the bank lobby.

I'm not going to scream. I'm not scared. I'm mad.

Maybe if she said that often enough, she'd believe it.

"Meet me at the Northwest corner of the gate," Asher yelled into his mic.

Her shoes crunched as she stepped on shattered glass. It was from the remains of one of the many huge pendant lights that had fallen from the ceiling. She couldn't believe how mangled the beautiful fixtures were —and that's when she saw a severed leg. It was lying three feet away from the oval bottom of the light. No body. Just a leg.

"There," she pointed as she gagged. Asher turned his head.

"Fuck." He squeezed her hand. "Stay here. And this time, do as I say."

This time she was more than happy to. Her vomiting was just going to slow them down.

When he came back, he said, "Bank employee." He

grabbed her hand and continued toward the stairs, next to the women's bathroom.

"Goddammit." Asher sounded pissed.

It was hard to see, even in the moonlight, what had him so mad. Then Eden spotted it—part of the wall was blasted. *It must have happened during the tank's attack.* The bathroom was exposed, sinks were hanging at odd angles. The door to the stairs was also blown open and Eden could see that the door to the outside was blocked by a huge beam.

"Maybe we can crawl over it," she suggested hopefully.

That's when she heard it. Commands in Spanish. The secret police were entering the building.

"We've got to try," Asher said grimly.

CHAPTER 11

He had to get her to safety. He *had* to. Never again was someone he cared about going to die on his watch.

He should never have let her try to help with the coward under the desk. Asher shoved harder at the beam, trying to lift it out of the way so he could get to the safety bar and open the goddamn door.

It was too heavy. He stepped back a moment and put his goggles back on. He needed to take a closer look at the door itself. That's when he saw the casing was now mangled metal that basically welded the door shut. Nothing but C-4 was going to get them out of there, and he heard the secret police getting closer.

"The vault," Eden said as she yanked at his arm.

"What?"

"We're screwed. We're either going to be captured and tortured or die. I don't like any of those options. To the vault."

Is she insane?

She yanked at his arm again.

"Explain," he demanded as he refused to move.

"No time." She started down the stairs.

Dammit, she knew he would follow her. And he did. As soon as her bloody shoes slipped on the stairs, he was there to steady her. He pushed through the door to the basement. She kicked off her shoes and ran down the hall until she got to the bars that encased the vault. She looked down at the keycode. She was scrambling for something in her skirt pocket.

Keycode! Rafa!

"Kane!" Asher yelled into his mic.

"He's busy. It's Leo. What do you need?" Leo's voice was a sea of calm.

"I need the gate to the vault opened. It's a keypad. Unlock it now. Then unlock the vault."

"Coming right up."

The longest ten seconds of his life ticked by, and then a green light came on the keypad. Asher shoved open the gate and rushed Eden inside. The gate crashed closed behind him. "Lock it, Leo."

"Done."

He and Eden skidded in front of the vault's combination keypad. "Open the vault, Leo."

"Wait a minute."

There was silence.

Asher saw Eden looking intently at a piece of paper in her hand.

"Fuck!" she cursed vehemently. *Nothing new in that.*

"What?"

"It's too dark. Give me your flashlight. I can't read Suzanne's writing.

He'd dropped it during one of the tank assaults. "Don't have it. What are you trying to read?"

"It's the combination to the vault. Suzanne gave it to me and Leland, said we might need to hide in it as a last resort," he heard the panic in her voice.

He reached into his tactical vest and pulled out a glow stick. He jerked off his night-vision goggles.

"Rafa doesn't have the combination," Leo said. "Trying to get ahold of Señora Azua at the hospital."

"Never mind," Asher said as he popped the stick and a green glow lit up the numbers on Eden's piece of paper. Her hand was trembling.

The door to the basement banged open. *Shit, I should've shot the lock.*

"You key it in," she said.

He did. It worked. The door was heavy. But he got both of them inside and the door shut before the enemy arrived and that was all that mattered.

"Leo, we're in."

No answer.

Asher tried again.

"Leo, we're in the vault. What's the status of everybody else?"

Nothing.

He looked around at his solid steel surroundings. Of

course, he wasn't being heard. In the eerie green glow, Eden grinned at him.

"You think that was funny, huh?"

"Yeppers. Did you figure it out?"

"You mean the fact that my radio won't work in here? Yeah, I think that's finally penetrated." He stifled a grin, waiting to see if she'd catch onto his stupid play on words.

She laughed. "Good pun. You know, I like you, Asher."

"Thanks, I like you too, Eden." And he meant it. Smart, good sense of humor in the middle of the madness, and she was willing to lay her life on the line for someone else. He shook his head and felt light-headed. Was it because of a possible concussion, or the woman in front of him?

Eden bent her head. He got the feeling that she was a little embarrassed. *Who would have guessed?* Then she looked up and smiled at him. "I gotta tell you, I really, really like the fact that there is carpet and a table and chairs in here. Suzanne has done this up right."

He held up the glow stick and looked around the large vault. It was huge. The entire back wall was covered with safety deposit boxes from floor to ceiling. In the middle of the room was a huge conference room table, with ten plush chairs. At the far right end was a door.

Eden sat down at the long table, in one of the plush armchairs, and reached under her skirt.

Reached under her skirt.

Reached under her skirt.

What the hell?

Then he saw she was rolling down one of her stockings.

It took all of his willpower to keep his tongue from rolling out of his head. She'd totally caught him off-guard with that move, and he hadn't realized just how much she'd turned him on.

Calm yourself, Thorne!

"These are shredded and covered in blood, I've been needing to take them off," she let out a tired sigh of relief as she stretched her toes.

He started to watch as she began rolling down the next stocking. She wasn't doing anything overtly sexy, but Asher still had to look away, or risk drool dripping on the carpet. The woman had legs that went on forever.

"No gold bars." He heard her yawn.

"Huh?" Asher hoped it was safe to turn back. It was.

"Didn't you always think there would be stacks of gold bars in a bank vault?" Eden asked. She yawned again as she stretched her neck. Instead of staring at the way her breasts thrust forward, Asher looked at the pile of silk on the floor.

"I think you're thinking of Fort Knox. The gold is probably in some of these boxes, not just lying around." He nodded at all of the numbered boxes surrounding them.

"Interesting," she mumbled.

He watched as Eden crossed her arms and lowered her head on the table.

"Tired?" he asked.

She shook her head into her arms. "No, not tired."

"Bullshit. You're exhausted."

Asher crouched down beside her. "It's okay to let go. Wind down."

"I told you, I'm not tired." She turned her head in her arms. "Am not." He had trouble hearing her, her voice was so low. "Just need…"

"Need what?"

Nothing

He waited for her to continue.

She closed her eyes, then opened them half-mast. "No more witty banter. It's done. Blood and body parts." Her voice trembled as she said the words. "I don't like this. I hated Maurice. Okay, hate's too strong of a word," she said as she closed her eyes, then opened them one more time. Tears shone in her eyes. "But no way in this world was he supposed to die."

Asher gently touched her back and felt her melt into his touch. He brushed soothing circles into her taut flesh as she continued to talk.

"Please don't be nice to me. I might totally break down. There's no breaking down for York girls, especially not me."

"What are you talking about? I'm about ready to have a meltdown, and I'm a SEAL. Are you special operations and I don't know it?" He teased low and gentle.

She pushed trembling fingers against her temples as her gaze shot over to look at him. "Cut it out, Asher. I know that game. I've played it. Just give me a minute. Just a second. Don't be nice to me, or I'll lose it. But if you give me a minute, I'll be good to go. I won't be thinking about either Estella or Grace dying." She tried to shrug off his hand, but he wasn't having it.

She was in need. He'd already let Xavier down; he sure as hell wasn't going to let this woman down too.

He looked at her confused expression. "You need to cut yourself some slack. I promise to only be nice and comforting for just a moment, then you can go back to being a York Girl." He pushed his fingers beneath her hair and kneaded the back of her head. Anything to give her comfort.

"Eden, almost everyone got out of the bank alive, you have to remember that. You were one of the major reasons they did."

"No, I wasn't. You and your team were." Her words were slow and slurred.

"You saved Suzanne."

"Raiden did," she protested.

"This argument is stupid," he muttered. He swung her chair around, so her bare knees were touching his chest. A mass of chocolate-colored hair tumbled around her face and shoulders. Asher plucked away the strands that were stuck to her tear-stained cheek and slid them behind her dainty ear.

Why was he surprised by the depths to this woman? All of the clues had been there. She couldn't have been that willing to put her life on the line without a deep well of compassion. Of course, she felt things deeply. Why in the hell would he once, fucking, again, think that someone who showed strength wouldn't need his support? How big of a dumbass was he?

Especially since he so dearly wanted to provide her comfort. He looked into the liquid depths of her eyes, trying to form a connection. Wanting to ensure that she was seeing into him as well.

"Truth. Can you see it? Hear it? Tell it?"

"I don't know." Her whispered words sounded so defeated. "I'll try."

"You've been amazing. You're the best thing that's happened on this operation. Your brother Pete couldn't have done better."

Her lip trembled.

"Yes, he would have. He would have caught on sooner about Carlson and Becker."

"Eden, will you look at me?"

Green eyes glittered up at him. "Seven hours ago, when me and my team started talking to you on the phone, you blew us away. You steamrolled right over Carlson who was supposed to be the all-knowing security on this caper. Then to find out he's the bad guy, but you still overrode him, is fucking amazing. You're all about protecting people, even at the cost of your own life. Who in the hell are you?"

Eden turned her hands in his and gripped them. She shoved her face into his so that they were damn near nose to nose. "I'll tell you who I am, one messed-up woman who is actually scared and sad. And I hate sad. And scared is the stupidest emotion on God's green Earth. It sucks!"

God, doesn't she know that this is the attitude that breaks you?

He released one of her hands and slowly reached up to cup her cheek. "You're absolutely right, mad is much better."

Her smile was all gritted teeth. "I knew you'd understand."

"But when scared and sad is what we're dealt, then we have to address it."

She took a deep breath. Her eyes searched his. Asher really felt like he'd gotten through.

She sat up straight. "I think my minute is done. What's the next step?"

Eden knew she'd taken him by surprise. What else could she do? The idea of falling into his arms and getting a hug from him overwhelmed her, and that was something *she did not do.*

Nope, not me.

But in her twenty-eight years, he was the first man who she ever considered leaning on outside of her family. How in the hell could her gut be telling her this damn fast that he could be trusted?

Listen up, girly. This is your heart talking, not your gut.

Eden grimaced. She really didn't need a freaking internal dialogue at this moment in time.

She snapped her fingers in front of Ash's face. "Come on little buddy, what's next?"

She heard him sigh as he stood up. She got that

reaction a lot from her dad and brothers. She ignored him and pushed up from the table, so they were side by side.

"What's next is, I see if my sat phone is working through all this concrete and steel."

"Chop, chop." She smiled up at him.

"You're incorrigible."

"I know. It's one of my most endearing traits."

When he pulled his satellite phone out of his tactical vest, he grinned. She caught sight of a dimple. "We have reception."

Eden gave a fist pump.

"Leo?"

"Jesus God, you're alive. Why didn't you call in sooner?"

She shoved her head next to Asher's so she could hear the conversation, then he hit a button so that it was on speaker.

"What's the status?" Asher demanded to know.

"I don't have names. But four of the five bank guards are out. Patel didn't make it, but Carlson did. We're missing one bank employee named Graciela Ramirez and three of the coalition."

"Eden's with me."

"Then two of the coalition."

"Maurice Schlessinger is dead, who else is missing?" Asher asked.

"Sharon Foster," Leo answered.

"Are any of your team injured or dead? Is Ezio hurt?" Eden immediately wanted to know. She thought about the hissy fit that Sharon had been throwing. Hell, she could have gotten other civilians and some of the SEALs killed with her crazy-assed behavior!

There was a pause before Leo answered. "No, ma'am."

She blew out a sigh of relief. And then she replayed her thoughts.

Oh God, I didn't just say that.

She started trembling.

Eden felt it coming again. It was welling up, like an unending tsunami.

"Ash," she started, then clamped her mouth shut.

"What is it?"

"She's the one I called screamy-meemy. Everybody I was mean and awful to, died."

I'm a hateful, judgmental bitch.

In less than a second, he had her hauled up against him, his lips in her hair. "Don't ever say that. Don't even think that."

"But they did, they died." If it weren't for Asher's arms, she would have crumpled to the floor.

"Not you. Never you, Eden. You saved lives." He held her tighter. It was as if he were trying to will the words into her soul.

"Asher," Leo called out.

Ash flipped a switch on the phone. "I'm here, what else is there?"

"It's a madhouse at the bank." Leo choked out a weary laugh. "Hasn't stopped Carnival, though. Nope, they're just taking their parade down another street."

"And us?"

"We haven't figured it out. The tank has backed out of the lobby and is now idling outside of the gate. The police are swarming the place like ants. They're crazy—the building is six stories high. The thing is not stable, they should get the hell out of there."

"Are they coming for the vault?"

"Like I said, they're everyplace. That includes the teller area on top of the vault. That area is stable, for the moment. Kane doesn't know how long that will last. It's the south side that's the problem. Kane wants to take it down. It won't hurt anyone on the street since it'd come down within the gate, but Max is all itchy. Everyone knows he wants you to be doing the charges."

Eden peeled away from Ash. She was good now. Tired. She was tired. That explained all the meltdowns. She felt him watching her as she drifted towards the huge row of safety deposit boxes. What was tucked away in each box? How many people's lives were tucked away in each individual box? It boggled the mind. *Lives.*

Sharon.

Maurice.

She should never have left Montana.

"...save the battery."

"Okay, check back in a half-hour."

"Will do," Asher agreed.

Eden looked over her shoulder to see Asher put his phone in its pocket on his vest, then peel out of his vest and rest it against the leg of the ornate wooden table.

"Eden, you need to sit back down and rest a bit. We're going to be here a while."

"How do you know?"

"Rafa explained this place is on a timer. It's not supposed to open until Monday morning. Suzanne is in surgery. Once she's out, they're going to try to figure out if they can override it."

"Hector?"

"What do you think?" Asher asked with a harsh laugh.

Ash was right, the bank manager was useless. She watched as Asher meandered over to where she was standing. Eden knew that he was being careful. Treating her like some kind of baby bird or something that would fly off.

"I'm fine," she spit out. "You don't have to walk on eggshells."

He stopped short. "Come and sit down, Eden. If there is one thing I've learned, you have to conserve your energy when you can."

She leaned back against the wall of safety deposit boxes, her toes digging into the red carpet. "It's kind of plush in here. Do you think it's so the high-faluting customers feel all special when they deposit their goods?"

"Could be," he answered slowly.

She looked all around the vault. "What's over there?" She pointed to a door.

"Eden." She recognized that tone of voice. It was a warning that she was pushing her luck. She really didn't care. She didn't want to rest. If she rested, she'd think. She wanted to know what was behind that door.

She pushed away from the boxes and stood straight,

and the room swam. She shook her head, trying to keep upright. Asher was there in a second.

She gritted her teeth as he helped her into one of the chairs and pushed her head between her knees.

"Take deep breaths."

"Go find out what's behind the door," she demanded.

"Don't be a brat."

She gave a weak laugh. "I've heard that before."

"I'm sure you have. But you're a beautiful brat."

"I haven't heard the beautiful part before, so I know you're full of it." He was stroking her hair and she enjoyed every moment of it. She felt tears starting to form, so of course she pushed his hand away. "Open the door, it might be gold bars. Inquiring minds want to know." She took another deep quivering breath.

"Stay put and I'll look, is it a deal?"

Eden didn't know if she felt cared for or shattered when his hand stroked her hair before walking away and trying to turn the doorknob. *Dear God, how is he burrowing in so deep?* He probably had no clue.

"It's locked."

"Of course, it is." She waved her hand at him. "Do your SEAL thing and open it." Out of the corner of her eye, she saw Asher grin. At least she was still a smartass. Points for her. But seriously, her body was crapping out on her. Eden lifted up and then rested her cheek on the flat cool surface of the table. The wood felt good. Maybe just a minute or two with her eyes closed and then she'd be back to her fighting weight.

CHAPTER 12

Asher caught her just before she slipped off the chair. How in the hell she lasted as long as she had was beyond him. Leland had told him that there'd been a crisis that had required her to work all through the night with NATO, so she was going on less sleep than he was.

The carpet might look nice, but it still was just cream on concrete. Asher wished he had something softer to place Eden on, but as soon as he laid her down next to the wall, she curled up like she didn't have a care in the world. *What would that be like?*

"Sweet dreams."

He looked at his watch. He still had eighteen minutes before check-in. What *was* behind that door? He went back to his vest and pulled out his personal utility pouch. Every one of the team had theirs configured a little bit differently. Asher pulled out his handy dandy lock-pick kit.

His main job was ordinance. He liked blowing things

up. He also liked disarming things. He'd been happy as hell when he'd read the term 'improvised explosive devices' in the ordinance manual. As far as he'd been concerned, that meant that it was his job to improvise a ton of shit. As the middle child, he'd been improvising his whole life. And since his job also involved blowing holes in things so they could get in and out of places, Asher had figured that meant he should figure out as many ways as possible to get in and out of places, hence learning how to pick locks.

He went over to the door and took a moment to examine it. It was a lever lock. He grabbed his curtain lock-pick out of the case, then it took him less than thirty seconds to get the door open. Too bad it wasn't as easy to unlock Eden's mind. There was so much that went on behind those witchy green eyes, it felt like his life and heart depended on finding out.

He snorted out a laugh. "Over the top, Thorne," he whispered to himself. "You are totally caught up in the dangerous situation."

He looked over at his shoulder at Eden and relaxed when he saw that she was sleeping peacefully.

He pulled open the door.

"Sorry, Eden," he whispered. "No gold."

It was a good sized room with table and chairs. Not nearly as ornate as what was in the other room, but still very nice. There was a credenza, a mini-fridge, trash can and two fake plants. They were certainly trying to impress people in here too. He opened the cupboards on the credenza for more of a clue as to what this place was.

When he saw the different trays and velvet tablecloths, he realized this was probably where people brought their valuables after they took them out of the safety deposit boxes. They probably wanted privacy away from bank employees.

He snagged the tablecloths and checked the fridge.

Score!

Still cold bottles of Fiji Water. Apparently, they liked to serve the good stuff to their bank clients. He couldn't have cared less what brand of water they wanted to serve. Okay, maybe not the previously used water bottles with the glued on tops with the germy local tap water that was sure to give you the runs. He'd gotten served that in a restaurant in Afghanistan and paid dearly.

He left the room with the tablecloths and knelt next to Eden. Slowly, gently, he lifted her head. Eden didn't stir. Asher put one of the folded cloths beneath her cheek then tenderly rested her head back down on it. The little moan that fluttered past her lips almost made him groan. Never had he heard something so feminine and enticing. God, he had it bad.

"Sleep, sweetheart. We're going to need the lioness soon enough." And wasn't that the damn truth?

He got up from his crouch and went back to the room so he could call Leo.

"Asher. What in the hell have you got yourself into?" his lieutenant demanded. "This is not the time to see if you can outdo Harry Houdini."

"You're showing your age, Max." Asher chuckled. "I think you're supposed to be saying David Blaine."

"David who?" Now Max was sounding pissed. "Shut the hell up and listen. Right now, it seems like you have half of Maduro's secret police force crawling over the bank."

"Good, I hope it falls in on them."

"Really?" came Max's sarcastic reply.

"Instead of an hour to blow my way out of here, it might take two," Asher blustered.

"Ah fuck, what do you mean?" He heard the defeat in Max's voice.

"Ah fuck is right," Asher agreed. "This thing was built in the fifties, back when they were thinking they had to withstand nukes. If I do any blasting from the inside, you won't find even a DNA sample of either Eden or me. Our best bet is having someone using the combination that Suzanne gave Eden or having a precision C-4 blast from the outside."

"What happens if it isn't a precision blast?" Max asked.

Asher chuckled. "Well then, a lot of those stupid fuckers of Maduro's are going to meet their maker."

"I appreciate the vote of confidence," Asher heard Kane McNamara chime in. "At least you knew that I wouldn't be blowing myself up."

Asher felt himself relax a little tiny bit at the sound of Kane's voice. Granted, the man wasn't as good with explosives as he was, but he was pretty damn good. If for some reason they couldn't get the vault open with fair means, Kane might be able to get it open with foul means....and C-4.

"Ezio says that his guy on Omega Sky is as good as you, and he's got him on stand-by to face-time me through everything. Of course, Ezio is probably just trying to talk up his team. Nobody is as good as you, buddy." Kane was pouring it on thick. "But I prefer waiting until Suzanne is out of surgery and getting the code from her."

"Why do we need her out of surgery?" Asher asked. "We have the combination."

"Ash, this is Kane. There's a teensy-eensy little problem. There is a revolving combination that's employed after each use. There has to be some kind of numeric code for Suzanne to remember, but we don't know what it is."

"How do you know?" Asher demanded to know.

"It's in the vault specs that Rafa pulled up."

"Fuck!" Asher gave a frustrated groan. "Just when you think something is going to be easy."

"My personal choice is Suzanne waking up and us finding out how to open that goddamn vault before the building collapses on it. Are we clear?" Max was still pissed.

"I love the sound of your caring voice, Lieutenant." Asher teased.

"Ah Jesus, don't go sounding like Cullen, otherwise I'll leave you in there. Now tell me how the civilian is doing."

"She's fine. Hell, she's more than fine. Did they tell you how she stepped up when needed?"

"Yeah, yeah, Leland can't quit singing her praises. He

told me that he would ruin my credit rating for life if I didn't figure out a way to bring her out safely." Max paused. "On a serious note, we should know about Señora Azua in about three hours. I've checked with the bank manager, Hector. He told me any kind of override rests with her. It's going to be a while before the secret police can dig their way to the vault to set charges, so unless you have a problem, don't bother checking in until midnight."

"I appreciate it."

Asher hung up and set his watch. That was one of the first things he learned, never pass up sleep, food, or water when it was available, because you never knew when you'd get a chance at it again. He picked up another velvet tablecloth. And a pillow, you never passed up a pillow if you had a chance for that, either.

How could Xavier look so calm? It never made any sense. None of it made any sense. Asher watched Xavier finish up scraping off the last dish in the sink, then put it into the dishwasher and start the dishes.

What the hell was that all about?

"Please, Xave, don't do this," Asher begged. He knew what was coming and it broke his heart.

Xavier ignored him. It was like he wasn't even in the room with his brother. Asher could see Xavier clear as day, but no matter how loud he yelled, Xavier ignored him.

"Please no, I beg you," Ash cried, his hands reaching out in supplication.

He tried to grab him, but his fingers went right through his brother's body. Ash looked down at his hands and realized that they were made of mist. But he had to try. He had to.

Xavier went to the refrigerator and pulled off a picture that had been taped to the front of it. The photo was of him and the men in the unit he'd served with when he was in Afghanistan. Xavier took it with him into the garage.

Asher followed, still yelling at his brother to stop.

"Don't go in there. Don't go!"

It hit Asher hard when he saw that Xavier's Mustang coupe and Triumph motorcycle weren't in the garage. Instead, a plastic tarp covered the cement. He knew this from photos he had pulled from the coroner's office. He fucking *knew this was how it looked.*

"Xavier," he pleaded. Begged. Cried.

His brother propped up the picture of his unit on his workbench. He picked up the Glock and knelt in the middle of the tarp. His gun was steady as he held it against his temple.

"I love you, Xave, no!"

"Asher, wake up."

"Don't do it!"

"Please, Baby, wake up now."

Soft, warm hands stroked his hair. A soft body nestled up against him. He kept his eyes closed, wanting to assess the situation before letting anyone know that he was awake. But he knew it was Eden in a heartbeat. Her touch and smell could never be mistaken for anyone else.

"Asher, it's a bad dream, please wake up." Her body was pressed against his, her arms wrapped around his neck. She whispered into his ear, coaxing him back from an old nightmare. One of his own making.

He reached up to pull her arms away, but she wasn't having it.

"No. I'm not letting you go."

"I'm fine, Eden." His voice was hoarse. He hated that.

"Bullshit."

He let out a dry laugh. "Warm and soothing didn't last long."

She sighed and settled closer. "If I thought warm and soothing would get my way, then I'd be all over it. It wasn't working. So just lie there and accept comfort."

Asher tried to sort out his feelings. He still felt sick at heart after watching Xavier's last moments on Earth. How many times had he relived that in his dreams? Then to wake up to an angel in his arms offering him the type of solace he'd never gotten before. He was having a tough time reconciling things.

"Ash?"

"I'm here now," he assured her.

He couldn't see Eden because he'd stuck the glow stick under his vest, so they'd sleep better. *Stupid.* Shit, he wasn't any better than a toddler who needed a nightlight, so he didn't have nightmares.

Her arms tightened around his neck again. She slid

her cheek against his jaw. "I don't know what you're thinking, but it's not good. So, stop."

He closed his eyes, trying to shut out the dark, like that made any sense.

"Talk to me, Ash."

"I can't."

"You just did," she teased gently. "Now say more words. Tell me about Xavier."

He blew out a shuddering breath. Eden was potent. She could comfort and stick a knife into you at the same time. Then he felt her fingers stroking his jaw.

"I can't," he said again.

"Whatever it is, it's killing you. We don't know what the next hours are going to bring. We're in this moment out of time, hidden from the world. Now will be the only minute you will ever be able to say your truth."

Every single word pummeled his heart.

She brushed the softest kiss against the side of his mouth. "I'm not even here, you're just speaking to your God."

Who made that sound? The one that sounded like a sob? Was that him? He took in a deep breath.

"Eden?"

"Hmmm?"

"The only reason I would talk, is because it *is* you."

She didn't respond with words. Just another butterfly-soft kiss that started at his lips and trailed down his jaw to his neck. Then she rested her head against his shoulder. "I'm here."

"Xavier is...was...the greatest man I've ever known.

He's my older brother. He was the rock that kept Lawson and me safe and sane when our dad died. He was there for our Maman to lean on. He was a hero in every sense of the word."

Eden just hummed her agreement as her body pressed even closer.

Asher pictured Xave's penetrating blue eyes and square jaw. "He joined the Army straight out of high school. It was another sacrifice—he hadn't been trying for a scholarship, he'd been taking care of Law and me, so he skipped college and just enlisted. He was golden and was almost immediately tapped for Delta Force."

Asher remembered the last picture that was taken with the three of them and their mom. He had it tucked away in his vest. It had been three Christmas's ago. The pride on her face shone through on the photo.

Eden stroked his jaw, and Asher realized he'd stopped talking. "Xave..."

She rolled on top of him. The darkness was absolute, but he imagined her green eyes staring down at him. Willing him to continue. He swallowed.

"Xavier came back from a mission and he was different. He received the Bronze Star for heroism. The deal is, you don't talk about missions, you keep it within the team or unit who was with you, but we talked. What the hell? We were both Spec Ops, and we're brothers. But we didn't talk about this one. Half his unit was wiped out on some Godforsaken hill in Afghanistan and he doesn't have a scratch on him, but the remaining men are treating him like some kind of Messiah."

Asher once again pictured Xavier, and how he looked when he came back.

"Eden, his body might have come back, but his soul didn't. I would look in his eyes, and I couldn't get him to really laugh, or really talk. He'd pretend and put on a pretty good show, but it didn't fool me. The only time he seemed real was when he was with another man from his unit. Then he was manic, over the top with concern, like he was their father or priest or something."

Asher must have been silent a while, because Eden prompted him.

"What did you do?"

"Not nearly enough. I tried talking to him. I went down to North Carolina three times, to try to get him to open up. Nothing."

Again, he must have stopped talking because Eden's voice was whispering in his ear.

"And then?"

"Then nothing. He killed himself. I fucked up. I didn't take care of my brother."

She pushed up on his chest. He could feel her looking down at him. Could she really see him?

"What else were you supposed to do?" she asked quietly.

"I should have reported my concerns to his lieutenant."

"Did you think he was going to kill himself? Really?"

Asher rolled and Eden was beneath him. Then he got up. He snagged his vest and the green light of the glow stick made both of them show up in stark reality. He gave a half-smile. "It's not our safe little bubble anymore. Talking time is over."

Eden clabbered up off the floor and shoved her fists on her hips. "Bullshit. Talking time has just started, Buddy. Answer my question. Did. You. Think. He. Would. Kill. Himself?"

"Fuck no. If I did, I would never have left. I would have tranq'd him, tied him up, and dragged his ass to the V.A. hospital," he yelled at her.

"Then what the hell are you blaming yourself for?"

"For being so stupid that I missed the signs. I thought he would end up fucking up his job. I thought he would end up being kicked out of the Army for not checking in, for dereliction of duty, and I wanted him to snap out of it because I knew how important being a soldier was to him."

"Did you want him to get help?"

"Fuck yeah, but I didn't think professional help was that important. I figured he could just pull himself up by his own bootstraps or just talk to me." He slammed the heels of his hands into his eyes. "I was so fucking wrong."

Asher was breathing so hard that for a moment he thought the vault was losing oxygen. Then he realized he was hyperventilating, so he took a couple of deep breaths.

"Eden, I had Kane pull the file on that damned mission. It was a freaking miracle that anyone survived. One of the Afghan fighters they were working with sold them out, they were surrounded. Xave's best friend in the Army died on that mission. When I read what he accomplished, I couldn't believe my eyes. Then I pictured it from Xavier's point of view—he would only focus on the twelve men who died, not the twelve men he saved."

Eden stepped forward and wrapped her arms around his waist. She rested her head on his chest, and he could breathe in the subtle hint of peaches from her hair. "What have you done since then?"

Ash tried to pull away, but she wasn't having any of it. "Answer the question, Thorne. What have you done since then? Since Xavier's suicide?"

"How did you know?" he rasped.

"I figure every hour together in a situation like this is at least forty-eight. So, I've known you for quite some time, Asher. Just answer the question. What have you done since Xavier's death?"

He pulled her closer, taking her weight against his body. She felt good. The fact that she had burrowed into his head and heart felt better.

"I've checked in with each member of Xavier's team, including taking them on a deep-sea fishing trip. I wanted to make sure they're okay."

"Were they?"

"All but one."

"What did you do?"

"I talked to his wife. We had an intervention and got him into counseling. He's doing much better now." This time, he did push her away enough so he could see her eyes. "How did you know?"

"I know you. I'm so goddamn sorry about your brother. I would love to have met him. But the man you were then did the best he could. You need to forgive yourself."

"I don't know if I can."

She sighed. "I can understand that. But try. Please try."

Asher swallowed. He blinked hard, but his eyes still stung. "I miss him so much, Eden."

"I know."

She twined her arms around his neck and pulled his head downwards. "You're a good man, Asher Thorne, and I just have to do this one thing."

Thank God. He wasn't resisting. Eden had been worried she might have a fight on her hands. Instead, he readily bowed his head and allowed his lips to hover over hers.

"Are you sure?" he questioned quietly.

She tugged harder.

Eden watched as a slow smile spread across his face. She shoved up on her toes and touched her lips to his.

Perfect.

Asher took over the kiss, brushing his lips over hers in a tantalizing slow rhythm that coaxed her into following. Slowly his lips parted hers, and his tongue stole into her mouth, seducing hers into a dance. She felt the sensations flow down her neck, into her chest, and tighten her nipples. She rubbed her breasts against his chest, trying to find relief.

Is that me whining?

Ash's fingers tangled in her hair, tipping her head in a way that allowed for a deeper kiss. She felt his heartbeat against her chest and beneath her fingers at his neck. He nipped at her lips, forcing her to open wider so that their breaths could mingle, and he could tempt her with a thrusting tempo, one that would be even more satisfying if it wasn't just his tongue and a kiss.

She moved her hands and scrabbled for the hem of his t-shirt.

"Shhhh, slow down," he soothed.

"No." She thrust her palms under his shirt and sighed with pleasure when she met with the hot hard planes of his stomach. It was like touching hot velvet steel, only better, because it was Asher. She needed more. She pushed up higher and then groaned as her fingers delved into his chest hair.

"God, Asher."

"Eden, you don't mean this, Honey."

She tugged at his chest hair to punish him for denying her. "I do."

"Eden," he protested.

"I need to get close. Just let me get closer to you." She heard the need in her voice and winced. "Please, Asher?"

As if he knew exactly how much it took for her to ask, he whipped the shirt over his head. It ended up somewhere, she didn't care where. Then she was lifted and gently lowered down onto the carpet, her head resting onto the makeshift pillow.

"I need to be close to you too, Eden. *You*, Eden York. No other woman would ever do."

How does he know the right words to say?

Asher looked her right in the eyes, then slowly, ever so slowly, unbuttoned the first button of her blouse. He placed a kiss on the upper swell of her breast. "So beautiful."

He trailed kisses upwards, until soon their lips met again, and she was lost in a maelstrom of heat, hunger, and passion. She tried to spread her legs wide so she could wrap them around Asher, but the skirt was too tight, so she had to suffice herself with squeezing his thigh. She pushed up against him, trying to ease her ache.

"Eden—" he started.

"I need more," she sobbed. After hearing his story. After seeing this man's soul, she needed him. It felt like the world was crashing in around them, and she wanted him! Was he going to make her beg?

"Shhhhh, I'm here." He cupped her head tightly to his chest. She started to relax. It was like she could breathe. "It's okay, Baby, I've got you. I won't let you down."

Is he talking to me or himself?

When he moved one hand and started undoing the buttons of her blouse, she stopped caring. Just this, the feel of his warm, calloused fingers touching her heated flesh. This is what she needed, to feel his touch and care as he caressed her nipples over the top of her lacy bra. She wiggled, trying to move her arms so she could take off her bra.

"I've got it handled," he whispered. "Relax."

How am I supposed to relax?

He pressed the joints in the backs of her shoulders, and she melted. Her arms turned to noodles, and he took the opportunity to divest her of her blouse. Soon he had the front clasp of her bra opened, and each breast was covered with his hot hands. *Glorious.*

"Do you like this?" She heard the confident tease in his voice. She liked it after the man had shared his nightmares with her.

"I love your touch, Asher. The only thing better would be the touch of your lips."

He laughed out loud, and so did she.

He didn't start with a kiss. No. Not Asher. His broad tongue licked her nipple and she nearly screamed. The silky, rough touch was earthshattering, and he did it again and again, and again. She couldn't stand it a second longer.

"Suck me!"

He laughed again.

"I like a woman who knows what she wants."

"Shut up and do it."

He blew on her wet nipples. She was in hell. She was in heaven. He licked.

"Asher, please. Baby, please."

He took her nipple into the hot cavern of his mouth and suckled hard. At the same time, his hand shot under her skirt and pushed away the crotch of her panties so that he could start another fire.

Eden was whipping her head back and forth, feeling the tug of Ash's fingers in her hair as his mouth teased and sucked at her turgid nipple and his other hand sought to kill her with pleasure as he traced the liquid folds of her sex.

She raised her knee, uncaring that her skirt was ripping—she would do anything to guide Asher's fingers closer to her clit. Again, she tried to move her hands so she could take off her panties, but he forestalled her.

"Uh-uh, what do you need, Sweetheart?"

"Panties. Off."

"That can be arranged." His words were nothing but smoky satisfaction. And like everything else about the man, it seduced her into a puddle of wanton need. Asher had her panties off in moments and her skirt rucked up around her waist.

"Touch me." She really wanted to say 'fuck me' but she'd never said that in her life. But she wanted to. She really, *really* wanted to.

"My way," Asher whispered against her breast. He reared up and caught her mouth in a torrid kiss. All thought left her as she felt his rough, canvas-covered thigh separate her legs. She moaned in pleasure.

He moved downwards, and then she realized what he was going to do.

"No! Not that. I want you inside me."

"I want to taste you. I want to pleasure you."

Asher continued to brush his fingers against her sex, and then slowly he pushed one into the well of her vagina and she clenched around him. She was so close to coming, she just needed a little more. Why wouldn't he just give her his cock?

"Asher, please."

He looked up at her. "I thought I was," he smiled.

"Fuck me!"

He bent his head and took a long lick around the base of his finger as he eased it in and out of her entrance. Eden shot up on the heels of her feet, anything to bring herself closer to the man who was giving her so much pleasure.

"You taste so sweet."

When he added a second finger, it took a moment for her to get used to it, but then the feeling was sublime. He pressed somewhere high inside of her at the same time his tongue circled her clit.

"It's too much," she whined.

He didn't answer. Instead, he suckled her clit and then lightly used his teeth to scrape at the sensitive nub as he inserted a third finger.

Eden scratched at the floor, at his arms, across his back, anything to ground her in the here and now, but she was lost. Everything that she thought was real had disappeared, left in the wake of the man who had rescued her and perhaps captured her heart.

CHAPTER 13

Eden tried to ignore the muffled beeping. Luckily, it stopped pretty darn quickly, so she was able to turn over, and that's when she realized she was plastered over the hot planes of a furry muscled male chest.

"Asher?" She winced at the panic in her voice.

"Eden?"

"Uhm."

"Are we going to have an awkward morning after?" She could hear the laughter in his voice, which woke her up completely. She sat up and felt the sway of her naked breasts. She looked down and saw that in the green light it was pretty clear that she was completely naked.

"Wait a blasted minute! I have a bone to pick with you! Why didn't we make love?"

She shoved at his naked chest, glaring at his pants that were still completely done up.

She looked up at his face and saw him biting his lip, trying not to laugh.

"Are you always this grouchy when you wake up? If so, I'm going to have to reconsider having a relationship with you, Ms. York."

"Answer the damn question, man."

Eden was seriously pissed-off. She remembered wanting to make love. Make *love*. Not have sex. Not fuck. Make love. Intercourse.

"Whatcha thinking? Looks interesting."

She swatted at his chest. "Just answer the question. Why did you deny me?"

This time, he wasn't able to stifle his laughter. "Good God, Woman. You had three orgasms then you fell asleep, how did I deny you?"

"I wanted to pleasure you. I wanted to pleasure us. Together. You know. Uhm. Together."

Asher sat up and pulled her naked form against him. "I know what you're saying. We had a problem. No condoms."

Eden reared back. That thought hadn't even occurred to her. How was that even possible? Oh yeah. They were in the middle of a Jason Bourne thriller and about to die.

"Oh yeah, condoms," she said weakly.

She needed something else to think about. Talk about.

In the eerie light, she saw that the door to the room was opened. She pointed to it. "Was it filled with gold?"

"Better than that. Water."

He handed her over a square plastic bottle that was beside them. "Drink up."

Eden turned the cap and greedily gulped down some

of the water. "Oh my God, this is wonderful. If you tell me that there is a bathroom in there, I will pay money."

"Damn, money. However, that's really not how I would like to be paid." He hugged her closer. "But unfortunately, there is only a trash can."

"I'm from Montana, I grew up hunting, camping, and fishing. A trash can is living the good life."

"Really?" She saw him peering skeptically at her in the green gloom.

"Okay, maybe it's been a while since I've camped, and maybe I've gotten used to hotels. But in this situation, I'm damned excited to hear there's a trash can."

He groaned. "Ms. York, you're about perfect."

"Why was the buzzer ringing?"

"Shit, I'm supposed to call in." He took a corner of the tablecloth and dabbed some of the water that had dripped onto her breast. "God Eden, you are every man's fantasy."

She tried to get a good look at his face, but he was staring down at her chest. He couldn't really mean that, could he? Surely this was just because they were thrown together, there was more to it than just serendipity, wasn't there?

"Buzzer," she reminded him. She needed to get her head on straight.

"I guess you're right." He leaned in and laid a gentle kiss on top of her heart, then lifted the vest that was propped up against the wall of safety deposit boxes, next to two makeshift pillows. Asher pulled his satellite phone out of one of the pockets and placed the call. He put it on speaker and watched as she hastily put on her clothes.

"It's Kane."

"How's the Señora?" Asher asked.

There was a long pause. Eden didn't like that at all.

"There was a complication," Kane finally answered.

"Just tell me. What happened?"

"Turns out, the bullet weakened her carotid artery. It was a miracle she got to the hospital alive. She hemorrhaged on the table. It took them a while to control the bleeding. She's finally in recovery."

"Is she going to be all right? I mean, are there going to be long-lasting effects?" Eden interrupted.

"No, nothing like that," Kane assured her.

"Then what the hell is your problem?" Asher demanded to know.

"You've got Maduro's men, or Perez's men, whoever the hell they are, trying to come at the vault from the top at the northwest side. They're not trying to come in through the front door of the vault, because that door is fucking secure."

"So?" Asher demanded. "As soon as Suzanne is good enough to talk, or write shit down, she can get us the hell out through the front."

Again, with a pause.

"Asher, we told you that the building is coming down on the south. Well, it's getting worse—now parts of it are crumbling in towards the vault. I don't know how much longer before it's going to hit the front door of the vault.

That's another reason why the secret police are coming at it from the north."

"How many of Maduro's men are there?" Eden asked.

Asher shook his head at her. "Honey, we're talking jeeps, a tank, and probably forty to sixty men."

"I think I need the trash can." She got up off the floor and went into the room. She didn't need to pee or throw up. She just needed a minute. One single, solitary minute. It wouldn't be the first time that she thought she was going to die. It was the second. Okay, there had been a few close calls running around the bank, but that was all the same part of this little clusterfuck.

No, that's not all. She remembered when she was ten years old and her daddy had to find her when she'd fallen off the side of Beecher's mountain and she'd ended up on that ledge for a day and a half.

Eden looked up at the blackness of the room ceiling. Well, she'd promised not to die then, because it would get her into trouble with her daddy. This time, *she'd* be pissed if she was going to die. So, it was time to figure out how she could be part of the solution. And, if that solution included making the best of the situation while they waited for their next move, so be it. Not only was she not alone on a ledge this time, she couldn't think of better company than the handsome SEAL waiting for her on the other side of the door.

Asher somehow managed to hold in a laugh. He knew it would be the lioness who would come out of the room. And there she was, striding barefoot and tall in her ripped pencil skirt and silk top, and she would *not* be happy if he chuckled.

This was the Eden York who had told him she had 'some-shit-plan' that was bound to work. He was pretty sure she planned to take on the tank and thirty of the secret police herself and leave the jeeps and the other thirty men to Asher's team.

"You're grinning at me," she jabbed a finger at his chest. "Stop your grinning, this is serious shit. What did you and your people decide?"

"That you should take charge."

That stopped her up short.

"Don't bullshit a bullshitter. You came up with some kind of plan, and I want to know what it is, and see if I approve."

Ash had not taken a seat at the table, instead piling up the tablecloths in front of the safety deposit box wall, making a nest for them. He held out his arm. "Come here."

"Why?" she asked warily.

"Don't you trust me?" he asked easily.

"With my life." She covered the space between them and knelt down beside him. He had his arm around her shoulders in an instant.

"A translator, huh? What else have you done?"

"I told you, I trained with my brother, Pete. I grew up

in Montana. I'm not a girly-girl if that's what you're thinking."

Asher snorted. "Uhm, Earth to Eden. You are too a girly girl. I've had my hands and mouth all over your girly parts."

"You know what I mean," she said as she snuggled closer. "Now, tell me the plan."

"The plan is, I'm supposed to call back in a half-hour. Right now, we've got eyes on the secret police. According to Kane, they don't know shit-all about explosives. What they're putting together is likely to blow backwards and do them a hell of a lot more damage than make any kind of dent on the vault."

"And how can he be sure, and how soon before that happens?" Eden demanded to know.

"That is the rub. Kane has been monitoring their channels. They're bringing in all of the pentolite and dynamite that they have from one of their coal mines. Apparently, when they bought their tanks and RPGs from Russia, they were shorted on the PVV-5A."

"They're bringing their what and dynamite and were shorted on their what?"

"Almost every country uses a different kind of plastic explosive. C-4 is the best, because we can mold it into a specific shape that will force the blast to where we need it to go. PVV-5A, the Russian version, does the same thing, just not as well."

"And that other stuff, the pennylight?"

"Pentolite is a step above dynamite, and a step down from plastic explosives. It won't get the job done for this vault. My guess is, Maduro's men are thinking that with enough of that shit, they can blow the vault."

"What will really happen?" Eden asked.

"A huge fucking crater with the vault falling into it, and people on the outside dying."

"And us?"

"The concussion in here is going to be bad. Real bad."

Eden gave him a smile. A real smile. "Okay. I understand now. Thank you. I really appreciate you not sugar-coating the smelly stuff."

She put her hand on his thigh and used it as leverage to push herself up. She walked over to the table, and Asher would bet his bottom dollar that there was more swing in her walk than was normal. She pulled out the chair at the far end of the table and then sat down on it and daintily crossed her legs. Then she put her elbow on the table, and chin in her hand. He wasn't absolutely sure because he couldn't see that well, but Asher was pretty sure she was batting her eyelashes.

"So, sir, do you have any food in that handy-dandy vest of yours? If not, I think I would like another bottle of that fine Fiji vintage, if you don't mind."

How in the hell can she make me want to laugh? He really liked the idea of a little make-believe.

CHAPTER THIRTEEN

"I don't have a menu for you, but I can tell you about today's specials." He picked up his vest, went back to the room and grabbed a couple of things, then wandered closer to Eden. Her skirt had ridden up high on her leg. He might not have been able to see her eyelashes, but he sure as hell could see her toned thigh. She knew it too, the little vamp.

"Uh-um. You were going to tell me something?" she reprimanded with a knowing grin.

Asher shook out one of the tablecloths and covered the table, then placed a bottle of water in front of her and bowed.

"Your drink," he said in French.

"Thank you," she responded in kind.

He grinned at her ease in getting into the game. "For the appetizer, I would suggest that you start with our wild seed option. It has a hint of salt, while providing that satisfying crunch for the most discerning palette." Asher rustled around in his pocket.

"Not sunflower seeds," she begged in English. "My brother Bobby lives on those, I can't stand them."

"I said discerning palette, Mademoiselle," Asher continued in French. "I would only provide the best options in such an exquisite establishment." He pulled out a baggie of corn nuts and Eden burst out laughing.

"Monsieur," she switched back to French. "I stand corrected. I should have realized that of course, you would continue to provide me with only the best this evening."

Asher's cock ached as he remembered Eden's naked body beneath his. But enough of that, now they were just having playtime.

Sex is playtime.

'Shut up!' he told himself.

This time, Asher was close enough to where he could see her eyelashes slowly close and open, luring him into her fantasy.

He poured out the corn nuts for her.

"Kind sir, are you going to dine with me?" Her French accent was perfect.

"It is my duty to first provide for the lady. For the main course, I would suggest one of our healthy options. There are four different flavors to choose from, each has a chewy cardboard texture base, layered with a sawdust cream filling that is then coated with a facsimile of either chocolate, strawberry, peanut butter, or mint. I must say, they are all very healthy and contain quite a bit of protein."

"I think a corn nut and strawberry pairing would go nicely together," her voice went up an octave as she visibly cringed.

"You are being too kind. I think you should leave that to me. I would suggest you go for the peanut butter and corn nut."

Eden's laugh was throaty. "Thank you. I will."

Asher handed her the protein bar, then settled himself down with the strawberry bar. He left the corn nuts for Eden.

"How do you speak French so well?" she asked in the same language after she took another delicate sip of water.

"My mother is from Belgium. I grew up speaking French and Flemish."

"But you're American."

"Yeah, Dad was Army Intelligence assigned to NATO. He met Mom there. According to him, it was love at first sight."

"And your maman?"

Asher grinned. "She needed a little convincing. She was young and was the baby of the family. The idea of marrying a foreigner didn't sit well with her."

"What was the age gap?"

"Eight years. Dad says their first date was horrible. He couldn't speak French worth a damn, and mom's English was almost non-existent. What was worse, her sister tagged along."

Eden laughed as she popped another corn nut in her mouth.

"I can top that. When I was fifteen, my dad sent out Eddie and Bobby on one of my dates."

"They were your brothers?" Asher guessed.

Eden nodded. "Bobby was seventeen and Eddie was nineteen. It was summer so he was home from college working the ranch."

"What the hell was your dad doing, letting you go on a date when you were fifteen?"

Eden laughed at the outrage in his tone. "You would get along with the men in my family, I can tell." She took a dainty bite out of her protein bar and immediately followed it up with some water. "So, Flyridge is a really small town. Mom and Dad are third generation, and I found out from the town librarian that Mom and Dad started dating when Mom was fifteen. Boy, Lori and Jenny were pissed that I got that information and not them."

"This I want to hear about. Mom's sister sat at the table with them. Did your brothers sit with you?"

"Our date was at the DQ. They sat in the booth directly behind Clayton. I could see them the entire time, but Clayton couldn't. I thank God for small miracles, but it was terrible. Bobby kept sticking straws up his nose, but Eddie just glared. He'd been glaring as soon as I came downstairs wearing my pink angora sweater. He told Daddy that he should make me go up and change."

"But he didn't."

"Nope, Mom stepped in. She said it was cute, and it really was. I was flat as an ironing board, so it wouldn't have mattered if it was three sizes too small—which it wasn't—it wouldn't have shown off a damn thing."

"Still, angora. And pink."

"Still, no boobs. It was amazing I was asked out. It was because Clayton needed help in Spanish class."

"Now, I don't want you to feel objectified or anything, but I might have noticed that eventually, you overcame the ironing board issue."

"I noticed that you noticed, Asher," she purred. "I like how you took your time thoroughly taking stock of my attributes."

Asher threw back his head and laughed. "Being thorough is part of the job," he was finally able to gasp out.

"Anyway, it took three more years before I was able to start luring boys in for realsies."

"I bet you had the whole school chasing after you. Were you a cheerleader?"

Eden snorted. "Not hardly. What about you? Athlete?"

"Nope, that was my younger brother, Law. I was student council and I started a group of us who would go volunteer at the local VA hospital." Before she could question further, he grinned. "I was really hoping to imagine you in a cheerleader outfit."

"You can imagine me in seven different bridesmaid dresses, does that help?"

He filched some corn nuts. "Depends how short the skirt was."

"Yeah, trust me, you wouldn't have been interested in me in any of those. Especially the tangerine-colored one. I don't know what Kimmie, my sister-in-law, was thinking. My sisters and I blame it on the pregnancy hormones. The next one I'm supposed to wear is green and purple. I'm going to kill my cousin."

"I want to see you in it."

"I'm never telling you when and where the wedding is happening, and I've bribed every friend and family member a good chunk of money not to post a picture of me on social media."

He was definitely going to have to put Kane on the job to find pictures.

She pushed the pile of corn nuts towards him. "I'm done. I'm savoring my main course." She held her protein bar in between her breasts. "This you can't have, the nutty flavor of trans fat coursing through my veins is too good to be denied."

"Here I was thinking about sharing, now I'm not," Asher chuckled. "Mine has the tangy flavor of high fructose corn syrup combined with strawberry seeds. It's to die for."

"Yeah, well," Eden said in English. She set down her protein bar. "Everybody wants a tasty last meal. At least the company is awesome."

Last meal? Did that just come out of my mouth? By the look on Ash's face, it had. She reached out and grabbed his hand. "I didn't mean it. We're getting out of here. I just let it get to me for a moment. I've got my head back in the game now. I promise."

"Ah, Honey, it's okay. This is a shit situation, you can have your doubts. Everybody does."

"I know, but I should remember that the 'only easy day was yesterday.'" Eden tried to smile.

"You know our motto?" Asher grinned.

She'd totally caught him by surprise. She liked that.

"I definitely have to know 'to liberate the oppressed' since that's the Green Beret's motto, and Pete is a former Green Beret. But I looked up the others, and yours stuck with me. There were days that I had to lean on it."

"I think everybody in the world has," Asher agreed.

"But now I'm living it in a SEAL mission way. Parts of this have been really fun."

Asher leaned his other arm on the table and stretched forward so that their heads were almost touching. "Do tell. What was the most fun?"

"Seeing Leland go all He-Man on Suzanne. Trust me, she's been Ms. Control throughout these talks. She didn't take crap from anyone. You know that she could easily have run this project, but she deferred to Heinrich. Then, seeing Leland do the Neanderthal thing and Suzanne allowing it, even appreciate it, that cracked me the hell up."

Asher's thumb rubbed against her palm, and he gave her an appraising look. "It only made you laugh?"

Eden opened her mouth to say yes, then closed it. Right now, in these circumstances, it wasn't the time for surface conversation. She thought back to Leland's behavior.

"At first it totally took me by surprise, you know?"

Asher nodded like he could understand. "And later?"

He was so close she could taste his strawberry breath.

"Later, I was relieved that he was taking care of her. Somebody needed to, and I was really, really, relieved that she had someone in her corner. A man." She said the last word with a reluctant grin. "You can't ever tell any of my family I said that it would ruin my rep."

"I promise."

Her eyes narrowed. "Hey, did you just sit up a little taller?"

Asher grinned broadly. "Well, I am a man, after all."

"Don't let it go to your head. What about you, do you ever have fun on these missions, or is it all scary adrenaline?"

Asher rubbed the bridge of his nose. "There was this one mission where for a week I was on thong patrol. That was both embarrassing and fun."

"You're going to have to give me a little more than that."

"There was an amateur singing contest in Europe that we had to babysit. They were worried about a terrorist attack. In order to fit in, we helped out the producer of the show, A.J. There was this one act that had a tendency not to wear their panties. Anything to win votes, I guess. I'll tell you, A.J. was pissed. But she had her hands full trying to herd those cats, so we helped."

"Poor you," Eden mocked.

"Yeah, it was a hard job, but somebody had to do it." Ash grinned.

"Okay, that was your best day, what about your worst?"

"I've got a better idea; tell me about your best and worst date. But you can't use this as your worst date, this is a gimme."

"Oh no, having dinner with you is one of the best dates I've ever had. You speak French, you're smart, you have a good sense of humor. The food sucks, and I'm not real thrilled with the ambiance, but the company? The company is outstanding."

"In that case, I *really* want to hear what your worst date was."

Eden pulled her hand from his grip and settled back in the chair. She crossed her legs and wiggled her back against the plush velvet backing to get really comfortable

"It was five years ago, when I was twenty-three. I really was a dumb bunny, just out of college—sure I knew everything, but oh-so-dumb."

"You went to college in Idaho, right? Were you still there, or had you moved back home?"

Of course, he knew about her. Probably had her resume memorized, along with everybody else's in the finance contingent.

"I moved to Boise to intern at the State Capital. My double major was Political Science as well as Animal Sciences. The Animal Sciences degree was to help out at the family ranch, but I wasn't eager to go home right after graduating, so I took the intern job."

"I like it. So, you knew how to deal with political animals."

"Sure, like I've never heard *that* joke before."

Asher threw up his hands and grinned. Yep, she made out a dimple. "Sorry, didn't mean to be redundant. But seriously, that's quite a dichotomy, what made you get into it?"

"I saw how the mismanagement of our land resources hurt the regular ranchers and farmers. I figured that if I could understand how the government was thinking and maybe play a small role in state politics, I could change things."

"Okay, how'd you come to be a translator?"

"Languages came easy to me. Mom was German, with a capital 'G'. Her maiden name was Minnewit, and when Grandma and Grandpa Minnewit came to visit from Iowa, they only spoke German. Then we had ranch hands from all over the place. Our foreman was from China, so I learned Mandarin. This was all before I was six years old. I even had Ernie Lai teach me the Mandarin alphabet."

"That's impressive," he tipped his head in her direction, but he kept his eyes on her face. "But back to the bad date."

"His name was Edwin. Not Eddie, not Ed, nope, Edwin. The third. I tried calling him Trey, that didn't go over either."

"You did that to get on his nerves."

"Well, when he comes out of the gate with all the rules about his name, hell yeah I had to poke the tiger," she grinned.

"So, this was a blind date, you hadn't met him before?"

"No," she sighed. "I told you I was a dumb bunny. This was the son of the senator I was interning for. The senator had set it up."

Ash put his hand over his face. "And you didn't find a way to get out of it?"

"Nope," she said succinctly. "I just blithely went ahead with it. I was rooming with another girl who'd gone to UI, so I wasn't too freaked when the senator had given my address for his son to pick me up."

Eden could tell from Asher's expression he was not happy with that little tidbit. "Yes, it felt a little weird, but it was the senator, and he was nice, so I figured it was okay."

"Not," Asher rumbled.

"Yeah, not," she agreed. "Now, I'm a farm girl, right? So, I don't have a lot to wear, but luckily my roommate had fixed me up with a nice blue cocktail dress. Good thing too, because he takes me out to the country club for drinks and dinner. But before dinner, there's cocktail hour with all the hoity-toity Boise. Not to say some of them aren't really nice, because they were. But Edwin wasn't. He referred to me as his father's typist. When I tried to object, he looked me dead in the eye and said, don't you get him coffee, Sweetie?"

"What could I say, I had. Everybody in the office had gotten his father coffee at some point in time. Whenever somebody tried to draw me into the conversation, he would say I wouldn't understand."

"*You* let that slide?" Asher asked in amazement.

"I didn't want to do anything that would ultimately upset the senator," Eden explained. "Then when we went to sit down for dinner, I found out we were with another couple. It turned out to be one of the partners from the firm where he was working. Edwin was just out of law school, but he was already trying to score points and work his way up the corporate ladder."

Ash raised his eyebrow. "And then?"

"This guy was with his girlfriend. They weren't

getting along, and he was ready for something new, and apparently, I was it. Edwin was happy to deliver."

"You're shitting me, right?"

Eden sucked in her lips and shook her head. "Nope. Wish I was."

"Somehow after dinner, we all ended up at Doug's house. It was when Doug was insisting on a midnight dip in his hot tub that I'd had enough. So had his girlfriend. Of course, neither of us had our cars. I called my roommate who came and picked us up.

"I was so upset. Then Edwin started calling me to say it wasn't what I thought that I had misunderstood things."

"Don't tell me you went out with him again?"

"I called Mom first. I needed her opinion. But first I got her to promise not to tell Dad. She gave me good advice, told me he was gaslighting me, trying to tell me what was actually happening wasn't the truth. She assured me that I was seeing things correctly." Eden snorted.

"What?"

"I screwed up by getting her to promise not to tell Dad. I should have said and don't tell my brothers, because within days, my oldest brother Pete was in Boise."

"The Green Beret?"

Eden nodded.

"Good for him."

"The day Pete showed up at my door after work, the senator had mentioned that Edwin had to be taken to the E.R. because he'd fallen down some stairs. Needless to say, when I saw my brother, I put two and two together right away."

"The more and more I hear about your family, the more I like them."

"Yeah, there's a lot to like," Eden agreed. "What about your Mom and brother?"

Eden jolted when an alarm went off. It was a timer on Asher's watch.

"Time to check back in," he gave a half-smile.

"If I didn't know better, I'd say you planned that."

"Then it's a good thing you know better."

He untangled their fingers and got up from the table. He fished out a can of Altoids and put it down in front of Eden.

"Dessert, Mademoiselle."

"*Merci.*" She smiled as she eagerly opened up the tin of mints.

"But beware, the mints aren't going to stop me from asking more questions," Eden warned. "But it was a good try."

CHAPTER 14

"This is Leo. We've got a problem."

"What else is new?" Ash asked. "Give it to me."

He looked over at Eden, who was frowning, so he put the phone on speaker and set it down on the table in front of her. He couldn't sit down. His blood was pumping too fast.

"Kane's got a lock on their communication's channel. He's been listening in to their conversations for the last hour. Señora Azua was right, Perez is in charge of this op. He's convinced there is a ton of money to be had in the bank, and he's cutting out Maduro, but nobody else knows that."

"If none of his underlings know it, how does Kane know it?"

"Maduro is still incommunicado, so this is all Perez. Our guess is that Perez is planning on looting the bank, then getting the hell out of Venezuela, never to be seen again. So, he wants this done before Maduro gets back to Caracas."

"So, what's Perez planning? It's Saturday," Asher looked at his watch, "at seven a.m. He's running out of time."

"He no longer cares if civilians know that he's trying to break into the bank. All sense of subterfuge is gone. The report on the news is that there has been structural damage to the bank, and now Maduro's people are trying to rescue bank employees. There's a news helicopter that actually live-streamed the tank blowing holes in the North gate so that secret police could get to the bank building."

"Everybody in Caracas would either believe them or would be too scared to say anything against them."

"Okay, so it's going to be an all-out assault against the vault," Eden said. "How are they planning on doing it? From what Kane said the last time, they only had dynamite and that other stuff."

There was a long pause before Leo started talking.

"Perez hasn't been talking about this on regular channels. He's been on his phone, so Kane hasn't been able to do his eavesdropping thing, which you know kills him."

Asher chuckled. "I wonder what A.J. thinks of that."

"You know she'd cut him off at the knees if he ever tried shit like that with her."

"I don't think that's what she'd be cutting." They laughed harder. "Okay, so Kane knows nothing."

"I didn't say that," Leo sounded like he was smirking.

"Would you believe there is an earthmover being unloaded outside the gate?"

"Hmmmm."

"Yep, they plan to dig their way in and then set the charges," Leo said. "But they won't work, will they?" Leo wanted reassurance.

"Leo, you need to keep an eye on things. They might not be digging just a hole for a man to climb down and set charges, they could be clearing the area so that the tank could shoot a mortar at the vault. Either way, it's a hell of an undertaking. It'll take hours."

"Or how about they're digging out a ramp so that the tank could angle its cannon at the vault and shoot at it that way?" Eden suggested.

Leo laughed, but Asher just rubbed his jaw.

"I see you trying not to laugh. They could be doing that. Wouldn't that give them a more precise shot? You know Perez doesn't want to destroy the contents of the safety deposit boxes."

"She has a point," Leo said.

"How is Señora Azua?" Eden asked.

"She's out of surgery. She's supposed to wake up on her own in two hours. If she doesn't the surgeon has okayed a shot of adrenaline."

What the hell? "Why not now?" Asher asked. They didn't have time to wait.

"He said it would be a bad mix with the anesthesia still in her system. They have to wait."

Eden stood up and put her hand around his waist.

"It's going to be okay. I swear, they're going to do the ramp. We have time."

"Asher, no matter what they're trying, we have time," Leo assured him.

"Yeah, but what you just said is that the bank has basically collapsed in on the basement. What's the assessment on us getting out through the vault door?"

Again, there was a pause. "Hold on, I'm patching you through to Ezio."

"Why—"

"Asher," Ezio started. "Nic, Raiden, and I are on our way to you."

"Okay," Asher said slowly. "How? What's available?"

"Not a lot," Ezio admitted. "The stairs from the lobby to the documents floor are non-existent. Kane blew a hole through so we could climb down through there. The documents floor has some crawl space."

Asher knew immediately why those three were the ones who were doing the crawling—they all had leaner body types than the rest of the team. Solid muscle, but leaner. "How far along are you? Is there any way to get some kind of protective gear for Eden to wear?"

"Already taken care of," Ezio said.

Shit, he should have known that. Still, he worried about Eden.

"We hope we can be there by the time Señora Azua wakes up to tell us the vault combination, but it's slow going."

"Be careful."

"Always." Ezio signed off.

"How much more juice does your satellite phone have?" Leo asked.

"About two hours," Asher told him.

"Turn it off for an hour and forty-five minutes. Nothing to be done in that time."

Asher hated the idea of being out of contact for so long, but when the real action started, he'd need the phone.

"Okay. I'll turn it on in an hour and a half."

"I figured." Asher could feel Leo's laughter through the phone line.

Eden had never thought she'd be so excited to savor a mint, but here she was trying to make the little candy last. And as stupid, stupid, *fucking stupid*, as it was, she wanted this time with Asher to last.

She remembered when it had come to the end for her Grandpa York. He'd been living at the ranch. He'd been on oxygen for the last two months of his life, and he talked to Eden a lot since she was the only child still at home. He said he wanted to leave the Earth having lived as joyously and with as much grace as possible. She'd always taken those words to heart. She just never thought that she might be faced with the possibility of dying at twenty-eight.

The mint was down to a nub. She looked in the tin and grinned. There were nine mints left. If the worst happened, then she and Ash would at least die with nice-smelling breath.

"What are you smiling about?"

"Nothing." She looked up and saw him staring at her. "Everything. This. You. Me."

"Well that clears things up," he said wryly.

She cocked her head. "You spend a lot of time laughing at me, have you noticed that?"

His brows drew up. "Huh, you're right. Maybe I should start calling you Cullen. Do you sing karaoke? Do you spend much time in Florida?"

"Nope."

"Still," he said as he made his way over to her, "you tickle me, Ms. York."

"I've done things to you Mr. Thorne, but I don't remember tickling being one of those things."

He shook his head, smiling. "Ah, there you go again. I'm entertained once again. And here we are without a deck of cards or indulging in sex. It's amazing. It's as if we like one another. Who'd have guessed?"

"You just set a low bar is all," she grinned up at him.

"Honey, if you're interested in tired old sailor like me, I'd say you're the one who has the low bar."

Eden plucked a mint out of the tin and stood. "Open up," she said as she held the candy against his mouth.

He didn't.

She swept the mint across his bottom lip, tempting him until he finally sucked it from her. But he held her fingers hostage, sucking them into her mouth. Her entire body went into meltdown.

Who cared about a condom? Really, in the big scheme of things, did it matter? What mattered was making love with this man. Asher must have seen what she was thinking.

"No, Eden."

"Yes, Asher. I refuse to possibly spend my last hours on this Earth depriving myself of something that I so dearly want."

"You don't know me," he protested.

"I'm twenty-eight years old. I've had three lovers in my life, and I can tell you unequivocally that I have never known one of them as well as I know you. All three times I thought I was in love, but the emotions you've pulled out of me make my feelings for them mere shadows."

"Eden," he sighed.

"Truth."

"I choose dare."

"That choice wasn't on the table," she admonished as she wrapped her arms around his chest and stared up at him. "Truth."

"All right. Truth."

"I'm not asking for love. That would be nuts. But a connection? Do you feel it?"

His hand came up and tucked her hair behind her ear. "How could I not?" He leaned forward and brushed his nose against hers.

Was she standing? Or was she now a puddle on the floor?

Maybe it was love.

"Do you want to know what I want?"

"Truth?" she asked, her voice trembling.

"Absolutely, truth."

"What?" she whispered.

"I want to hold you in my arms while you tell me all about Montana. I want to picture you growing up on a ranch with your daddy and mom and brothers and sisters. I want to hear what it was like being the youngest York girl."

All the time he was saying those seductive words he was guiding her back to their little nest of tablecloths. Soon they were settled down and she was safely tucked in beside him, her head resting against his chest, his arms around her.

"What do you want to know?"

"Everything. Anything."

Eden didn't just tell him about her family, she painted pictures in his mind. He could see what her childhood was like on the Montana ranch. The York men were big and gruff, starting with her grandfather down to her brothers, but the biggest influence was her father. The town sheriff. She explained how most ranchers had to have a second job to keep a ranch afloat in Montana, but for her dad, serving the people was a calling. He believed in justice and helping the people of his community.

If Richard York was the solid rock foundation of the family, then Heidi York was the soft landing for her husband and children. But while she always provided the comfort and good cooking that her family needed, she never shirked her duty as a rancher's wife, and Eden explained there wasn't a chance in hell that the family business could have thrived like it did without her sure hand at the tiller.

Then there was the ranch itself—eight thousand acres of cattle, with a little less than two thousand head of cattle. There was the cherry orchard that had been planted by her great-great-grandfather and was definitely Heidi's domain. The family revolved around the ranch, and it gave them a sense of pride, instilled ethics and honor, and taught them the value of hard work and teamwork. It was a good way to raise a family.

"Don't get me wrong, there were lean years, and we wouldn't have survived without Daddy's salary as sheriff. Hard winters where calves died, or strong winds that damaged the cherry trees. But we learned not to whine and just make the most of what we *did* have."

"Did that make it tough at school?"

"You mean because I was wearing hand-me-downs of hand-me-downs? Nah, everybody knew not to mess with me, because my brothers would take exception."

Asher raised his eyebrow. He wasn't stupid—he'd had a girlfriend in high school—he knew how vicious the girls could be, all without lifting a finger.

"Fine, it wasn't always fun, and there were mean girls," Eden admitted. "Plus, I was considered *teacher's pet*, because I was smart. But my brothers and sisters were my best friends...finally. Lori and Jennifer were eight and ten years older than me, and they were always great big sisters because they had done all the shitty sister stuff to one another. By the time I showed up, they were just supportive and nice. Bobby had grown out of his asshole-brother stage by then."

"But you didn't tell me about school," Asher prompted.

Eden pushed against his chest so she could look into his eyes.

"But I did," she protested. "School was just a jumping-off point for college. What mattered was my family and the ranch. Yeah, I made some friends, had some dates, but anything that was negative mostly rolled off my back. Hell, by the time I was a freshman in high school, Pete had come back home with part of his leg missing. How could I ever think that some mean girl bullshit was important after that?"

Asher couldn't help himself. He hugged her close. "You amaze me."

"There's nothing amazing about me. Now, my family, my parents. *They* are the amazing ones."

Behind her back, he looked at his watch. They still had a half-hour before check-in time. Asher bent in for a kiss, but she shoved at his chest.

"Uh-uh. Now it's your turn."

He rolled his eyes heavenward. "I told you about Xavier. My mom is different than yours. You hit yours with anything, don't you?"

"Definitely," Eden grinned.

"Maman has been hit hard by life, losing her husband when her boys were, ten, twelve and fourteen and she was trying to hold down a job in a foreign country. But she managed."

"I don't know, that sounds a lot like what my mom would do."

"But the woman she was, shut down. We didn't have her for a couple of years. Don't get me wrong, she functioned brilliantly. Never once did she start leaning on us, she was always Maman. But her heart was missing. Not mean or anything, but not the woman we had grown up with. But when Xavier left for the Army, she snapped out of it. It was like she realized that she wasn't experiencing her time with her sons. I feel bad that for the last four years he was home he missed out on her spark."

The entire time he'd been speaking, Eden had been drawing circles on top of his t-shirt, providing him comfort. His lioness cared.

"And Law?"

"God, I'm worried about him. He's so angry. He doesn't talk."

"Like you?" she asked softly. There was no hint of a smirk, which he would have expected. Then he realized of course she wouldn't. Underneath the hard smart-ass exterior was a soft, compassionate creamy center.

"No. I've talked to some of my teammates, and I've done a lot of reading on the subject so I could wrap my head around why he did what he did. I also talked to one of my old psych professors from college to get some perspective."

"But have you really made peace with it?" she asked.

"No, and I never will. But do I forgive him? Do I love him? Am I not angry anymore? Yes, to all three."

"Peace is hard to come by. What would get you there, do you think?"

"I don't know. I really don't know. But not being angry, that was big."

"How is your mom handling it?"

Shit. She had to ask that, didn't she?

"She doesn't know. I lied to her. She lives in Belgium now, I didn't see any reason with burdening her with the fact that Xave killed himself. She's had enough in her life without knowing that."

Eden's arms clasped him tighter and she kissed the middle of his chest.

"You don't have anything to say about that?" he asked.

"Sweets, you know your mother better than anyone. You know what's best for her." He loved her confidence in him.

"Tell me about your brother Law."

"When we get done with this mission, I'm taking some leave and going and kicking his ass."

She looked up at him again. "Pretty sure of yourself, aren't you?"

"I'm pretty confident in my team getting us out of here. We're getting out of here, no sweat. But kicking Law's ass? We're kind of evenly matched, we both might end up in tatters."

"So, why are you kicking your brother's ass?"

"He is *not* dealing. He's angry as hell, and he can't get

over it. He can't even get to the sad part. He's torn up inside. I want him to see someone. Anyone."

He looked at his watch. It was time to check in.

"Showtime, Eden. Are you ready?"

She took a deep breath. "Always." She untangled herself from Asher and got up. "Need help?" she asked as she held out a hand.

"I think I've got this," he smiled.

CHAPTER 15

"Ash, it's Max."

Asher braced. It was coming down to the end if Max was coordinating everything. "Okay, what's the deal? What do I need to do?"

"How much power do you have left on your phone?"

Asher looked down and did a quick calc. "About an hour and ten."

"Okay, put it on low battery."

"Uhm."

"Scratch that, stupid suggestion, it's already on low battery."

"Yep, whenever I call out and can get a signal, it's been on low battery," Asher said.

"We're estimating that the Venezuelans will be done digging at the back of the vault in another hour. Ezio is thinking he'll be at the vault door in less than fifteen minutes."

"Ezio? What about the rest?"

"He's a crazy rock climber and caver on his off-time. He's making great headway getting to you. He's leaving Raiden and Nic in his dust. Literally." Max muttered the last word.

"And Suzanne? Did she wake up?" Eden asked.

"Yes, Ms. York, she has. The adrenaline caused no adverse effects. She was able to talk to Rafa and explain what needed to be done to open the vault from the outside."

Asher felt like a thousand-pound weight had been lifted from his shoulders. *Talk about close timing.*

"Ezio will call you as soon as he gets to the vault door. In the meantime, keep the phone on."

"What about the rest of the people? Becker and Carlson? Do you have them locked up?" Eden demanded to know.

"They're not going anywhere at the moment. We're not taking off on the plane to Puerto Rico until you're rescued."

"That wasn't my question," she bit out. "I want to know if you have those assholes locked up. They're evil. Especially Becker."

"That's not our job. That's for a court to decide."

"But—"

"Ms. York, that's how it is."

Asher could see the steam coming out of her ears. He squeezed her shoulder, but she shook it off and glared at him.

"Hold on, Ezio is coming through on the radio."

Asher strained to listen, but he couldn't make out what the man was saying. Finally, the talking stopped.

"Did you hear that?" Max asked.

"No."

"He's at the gate to the vault. It's been destroyed. It's wedged against the door of the vault."

Asher and Eden looked at one another. Asher remembered just how sturdy that steel gate was. "I'm hanging up now, Max. Have Ezio call me."

"Yep."

It felt like forever before his phone rang. Eden had a calm look on her face, but he knew it was bullshit because her hand on his forearm might possibly leave bruises.

"Asher," Ezio said before Asher could say a thing. He sounded out of breath. "How are you doing?"

"Hanging in there."

"Damn glad to hear it. We're going to get you out of there, don't you worry."

"I wasn't worried until you told me not to worry," Asher said sarcastically. "Your bedside manner sucks."

Ezio huffed out a laugh. "Cut me some slack, man. I've been sweating up a storm trying to crawl through this maze."

"Don't bitch to me, you do this for fun. You're just getting a chance to do your weekend workout on the job, so be happy."

Ezio laughed again. "Right now, I'm going to try to crawl under the gate to see if there is any way I can leverage it up off the door. I'm hoping there's something underneath the gate that I can shove up under it. If I was a really good boy this year, maybe I can find something to use as a fulcrum."

"We can only hope."

"Hanging up now." Asher's phone went dead. He quickly tried to think of something to take Eden's mind off of their predicament.

"What's your friend Kane doing right now? Can we get him on your phone?"

"We can try, but I'm betting he and Cullen are securing some transport other than a food truck to get everybody to the plane, or they have eyes on what's going on with the secret police to keep Max and Leo appraised of the situation."

Eden's expression was fierce. "I need Kane to let Leland know everything he's found out about Becker. Leland will be able to have everyone coming down on him like a ton of bricks as soon as he hits Puerto Rico."

"He has that much power?"

"Oh yeah, he can get that done. I don't want Becker disappearing into the wind."

"Let's make this fast." He got Max back on the phone and explained the situation. It was like Asher thought—Kane was a block away from the bank on a rooftop, keeping watch on the secret police's operation. Max promised that Kane would call Leland from his current position and fill him in with the details.

What?

Asher almost lost his footing as the vault shook.

"Ouch!" Eden yelled.

"Eden, what's wrong?"

"Nothing. I bumped hard into the table. What was that sound? Why did the vault move? Was it Ezio? Is he okay?"

"No, it came from the safety deposit wall."

Asher called Max.

"What was that?"

"What was what?"

"Something just felt like it hit and shook the vault. Did they hit us with charges?"

"Hold on, I'm getting a report from Kane."

He and Eden looked at one another.

"It was the earthmover," Max said. "It slid down into the hole it was creating. According to Kane, one of the secret police was operating it."

"You've got to be kidding, who manages to do that?" Asher exclaimed. He turned to Eden, "There goes the possibility of creating a ramp for the tank to go down."

"Huh?" Max said.

"Never mind," Asher said. "Check with Kane, see if they are going forward with the dynamite and pentolite."

"Will do. Ezio briefed me on the problem with the door. He and the others will get it figured out, don't worry."

"Don't tell me not to worry, it makes me worry more."

"Fair enough," Max sighed.

"Hey, I just thought of something," Eden interrupted. "We said that the concussion would likely kill us if they did the dynamite thing. What would it do to the safety deposit boxes?"

"It'll blow up the ones that are directly near the blast, but the others will be fine," Asher answered.

"How big of a hole are we talking?" Eden wanted to know.

"If they're smart, no more than two-by-two meters."

They both looked over at the huge wall of boxes and realized that would leave hundreds of boxes intact, if not over a thousand. It would be worth it.

"How soon will they get it done?" Eden asked Max.

"Ms. York—"

"All things considered, can it with the Ms. York and call me Eden. Will Ezio get the door open before they blow us up?"

"Absolutely. Kane and Cullen are trained snipers. As soon as they look close to having this put together, they're going to hit the dynamite before they get down in the hole."

Asher grinned. He liked it. Still, he'd like to be out of the vault first, just in case they couldn't get off the shot.

"Nic said he's trying to call you. Need to hang up now."

He did, then his phone immediately vibrated. It was Nic. "Yeah?"

"We have a plan. Raiden and Ezio found a piece of rebar that they plan to use as a lever. Part of the gate twisted, so they can use that as the fulcrum. They really think they have a good shot of getting the gate pushed away for a minute, maybe two. That's all the time you'll have to squeeze out when I put in the passcode. We need you ready as soon as the door clicks open."

What Nic wasn't saying was, if they lost the battle holding the gate, he or Eden could be crushed as the door slammed shut.

"Got it."

"I'm keeping the line open, so you know what's going on."

"Good."

The kid hadn't put his phone on speaker, and that must be Raiden's doing. Apparently, this was not a good situation.

"Got your shoes?"

Eden pointed downwards. Ash nodded in approval. "They've brought something better for you to dress in as you climb through the mess to get to safety."

"You guys really are Boy Scouts," she teased.

"I was an Eagle Scout, ma'am." Nic's voice was proud.

"How stable is the building out where you are?" Asher asked, just killing time.

"Nothing moved while we were spelunking. I might take this up as a hobby. Ezio says he'll take me caving sometime."

"Great, now you're going to—"

"They've got the gate moved. I've put in the code and I'm opening the door."

Asher had Eden positioned to go first.

He could see Nic through the door, straining to keep it open. Shit, it was going to be a tight fit even for Eden.

She saw it.

"Asher?" she looked back at him.

"No time," he said, as he started pushing her through.

As he squeezed through a little bit, he could see what Raiden and Ezio were doing. It wasn't looking good. He shoved her hard into Nic's arms.

"Raiden?" he yelled.

"Gotta hurry, man."

"You gotta give me more room."

He started through, trusting that his team would make it happen. His head, left shoulder, and left leg were in, but there was no way his chest was going to make it.

"Three inches, I just need three inches," Asher called out.

Asher was sweating bullets. He might trust his team, but what happened if the rebar snapped?

Happy thoughts. Happy thoughts.

He pushed at the door, trying to help. *Did it just move?*

"Now!" Raiden cried out.

The door gave another two inches at most. Eden grabbed his left hand and yanked. He pushed off on his right leg. His shirt tore.

"Thorne!" Raiden shouted. "Now!"

He shoved for all he was worth.

Asher actually felt the door snip at his boot as it slammed shut, but he made it. He made it.

Eden still had his hand gripped in both of hers as she was sitting on the rocky floor. Raiden, Nic, and Ezio were holding a snapped piece of rebar.

Talk about a team effort.

"You good?" Raiden yelled over at him.

"Good as gold."

Raiden chuckled at his pun. Eden didn't.

She grabbed him around the neck and gave a rebel yell.

All four men laughed, albeit tiredly.

Eden gratefully pulled on the jeans and the long-sleeved sweatshirt that Nic handed to her. The clothes kind of fit, and that was all that mattered. They had even gotten her a pair of gloves and some Venezuelan version of Skechers that didn't come close to fitting in any way shape or form, but the thick socks were a Godsend.

She looked Raiden and Ezio over to see if they were all right. She'd seen her brothers after they tried to do something stupid like prove to each other who could lift a tractor tire, but these two men didn't even look out of breath.

"Eden, you're going to be behind me. I'm going to go slow, but Asher will be behind you so he will tell me if you're getting tired."

She nodded. She hated to admit it, but sometimes she pushed too hard and then ended up in a heap. It was good that they would be watching her. On the smart side, she'd been staying hydrated, so that would help.

"Raiden and Nic, you're taking the rear. Any questions?"

Everybody shook their heads.

"Let's get moving."

Even the first little bit was hairy. They had to climb over the gate, but pieces of rebar were sticking up from underneath, and it was sharp. Ezio was good—he pointed out every single movement he made, where to put her knees and hands when he was crawling, and where to put her feet when she was shimmying through tight spaces.

"Do you coach caving?" she yelled, her breath labored.

"Hold up," Ezio said into his mic.

"Why are we stopping?"

"I need some water. So, do you." He was such a liar. He'd heard her gasping for breath. She shouldn't have talked.

As soon as he handed her a canteen and she took a slow sip, she didn't care how big of a baby she was, she was just grateful. She couldn't tell where they were exactly, because the documents room had caved onto the basement vault floor, and there were gaps higher up where the marble lobby floor had collapsed.

"Where are we going?"

"We got in through the west door on the third floor. We had to climb down the wreckage to get to the basement, but the door itself is now open."

"West. Is that the one near the ladies' bathroom?" Eden asked.

"Yep."

She took another sip of water and went to hand the bottle back to Asher, but he held up his canteen. "Nic provided," he explained.

She gave hers back to Ezio. "Okay, I think I'm ready."

"Okay, because here's where it gets a bit tricky."

"Oh, great," she mumbled.

Asher stayed inches behind Eden as Ezio took them up and over some crumbling cement and rebar.

"I don't remember this being such a far walk from the vault to the ladies' room," Eden quipped.

Then she slipped back a little bit into Asher. "Or as treacherous."

"It's okay, we've got you covered." He held her for a moment as she took a deep breath. Ezio had stopped and come back a couple of moves so he could show her again how to navigate the path.

"Thanks, guys, I've got it now."

"We're almost there."

"Then we just have to get past the secret police, right?"

"Carnival is still going on, they've just steered it around the bank. We're still going to use it as a cover. Don't worry, we have a plan."

"A plan-plan, or a some-shit-plan?" Eden asked. "Because a some-shit-plan is usually best in these types of circumstances."

"Ignore her," Asher advised Ezio.

"We need to get going. It's not too much further. And it's a plan-plan," Ezio told Eden.

"Ow." She cried out, then tried to cover it with a laugh.

Asher saw what had happened—her foot had stepped on exposed rebar.

"Stop!" he roared.

"It's nothing," Eden protested.

Asher grabbed her ankle so that he could see her foot. Some blood was showing on the outside of her sock. He gently pulled her shoe and sock off and saw where it had sliced a two-inch gash along the inside of her arch. At least it wasn't on any of her pressure points and it wasn't a deep cut. He heard shuffling behind him. He didn't need to turn around to know that Raiden and Nic were changing places.

"Move," Raiden said.

"You've got a med kit?" Asher asked, since his teammate wasn't carrying his backpack.

"It's in my utility pouch." Raiden had already pulled out some antibiotic ointment, bandages, and gauze.

"Damn, Eden, I thought I might be able to do a little sewing here in the darkness and rubble, but you didn't cut it deep enough," Raiden teased.

"I'll try harder next time," she promised.

As soon as he was done, he scooched back behind Asher and resumed his position at the back of the line.

Asher stayed as close as a flea on a dog for the next forty-five minutes it took to get them to the door. Of course, there were no whimpers coming from the York camp. *Nope, not from my girl.*

Ezio immediately checked that the door could still open when they reached it. It could. All five of them huddled close to freedom, Asher holding most of Eden's weight, so she didn't have to put it on her foot.

Cullen had been talking to their group on and off for the last forty-five minutes, promising them that he had a plan-plan to get them safely to the Azua hacienda.

"If it includes a food truck or a parade float, I'm not interested," Asher gritted out.

Cullen laughed. "I think you'll like this. It's got style."

Even though Asher had his radio on speaker for Eden's sake, he knew she couldn't hear it in the confines of their 'cave'.

"I don't care if it's a party limousine, how in the hell are we going to get past all the secret police?"

"Kane has a plan-plan," Cullen chuckled.

"Lyons, quit being coy and fill us in," Asher damn near shouted.

"I would if I could. But first, everything has to happen the way we need it to. So, just sit your happy asses down for five minutes, and let's just see if everything works out the way we think it will."

"Well, tell me this—do you have a back-up plan?" Asher asked sweetly.

"It involves a food truck."

Asher stopped asking questions.

CHAPTER 16

"I'm not going to drive up until the explosion. I don't want anyone looking your way. Ezio, you know that the only reason they've stayed away from this entrance is because part of the wall fell on that truck, so everybody thought this entire wall was compromised."

"Only because it is," Ezio ground out.

"Don't be a whiner," Cullen chided.

"Anyway, I'll tell you the second I'm driving up. We have to wait until Kane and Max do their diversion."

"What's that?"

"They still haven't gotten to the point where they can deploy the dynamite and pentolite. So Max is on recon to find out where they've stored the explosives. If he can set charges without getting himself killed, great. If not, then they'll arrange for a grenade launch."

"Got it."

"Be ready."

"The story of our lives," Eden muttered.

Asher looked down at the woman at his side and pulled her in even closer. They needed to take this fast, but easy. Ezio caught his eye and sidled over to Eden's other side. She gave a put-upon sigh when he eased an arm around the other side of her waist.

"I hate being an invalid."

"Suck it up, Woman. We've all been there," Ezio admonished.

"Can you hear me?" Max whispered through their receivers. Ash turned his up so Eden could hear.

"Yep," Asher answered.

"Got the explosives targeted. Kane's going to Cullen. I'm taking the shot. I'll do a countdown after Kane gets to Cullen."

"How are you getting back to the hacienda, Boss?" Cullen asked.

"I'll figure out something. If I'm late, you men get the coalition members to the plane. Do you understand?"

"But—" Eden interrupted.

"Not now," Asher shushed her. "Trust Max."

They all heard the roar of an explosion through their receivers. "Bullseye," Max's voice was filled with satisfaction.

"I'm almost to Cullen, he's at the doorway," Kane said.

"Come out," Cullen yelled. "I'm in the ambulance."

The back doors of the ambulance were being flung open as they came out the door and ducked under a portion of cement wall. Eden stumbled but Ezio and Asher kept her upright.

"We've got company," Kane yelled as he knelt down alone on the right side of the vehicle. He aimed his MK 46 and started shooting at the oncoming men. Cullen was inside the ambulance and he pulled Eden in as Ezio and Asher threw her at him.

Ezio turned to get into the firefight with about eight to ten fighters headed at them, but Raiden and Nic were already in it, their rifles making mincemeat of the secret police.

The shooting was dying down. "Up!" Ezio yelled to Asher. Before he could comply, he saw Kane take a hit. *Must have been a sniper*, he thought as he ducked under the door to help Kane.

"I'm fine," Kane said as he pushed up from the ground. His shoulder said otherwise.

Asher pulled Kane back under the door. Nic and Raiden were in the ambulance with Eden and Cullen. Ezio helped push Kane up into the back. Asher and Ezio got into the vehicle and rushed to shut the doors.

That's when Asher felt the bullet hit him. He flew backwards into the ambulance.

"Asher!" Eden screamed.

Dammit.

He felt her arms clutching at him. "Someone help him."

"Eden, move out of the way." It was Kane's voice.

He felt ripping. Someone was cutting at his shirt and his pants.

"Jesus," Kane said. "Raiden, I need—"

"Got it right here," Raiden answered.

"Asher, hang on, Baby." Eden's voice.

"I'm fine..." Asher tried to say more, but the darkness took him.

"I'm not getting on the plane until you tell me where you took Asher." Eden refused to go up the steps. She was the last person of the coalition to get on the small plane that was going to take them to Puerto Rico. All along, Max had been promising to give her an update. At this point, it was clear he'd lied.

"He's going to be fine, Ms. York."

"I demand you tell me where you took him. I demand to know how he's doing."

I'm not going to hit him.
I'm not going to scream.
I'm not going to cry.

"That's classified. You can trust that he and Kane are getting the best care the US Navy can provide."

I'm not going to hit him.
I'm not going to scream.
I'm not going to cry.

"I don't really care, now do I? That wasn't what I asked. Let me be clear, since you obviously are not understanding me. Where did you take him? How is he doing? What is his prognosis? When can I see him?"

"I'm not at liberty to divulge any of that information to you, Ms. York."

"My name is Eden."

"Ms. York, I need you to get on the plane."

Gently, Lieutenant Max Hogan broke her grip on the handrail of the stairs. He looked over her shoulder.

I'm going to hit him.

I'm going to scream.

But I'm still not going to cry.

"Explain to me why I got to know everything about what was going on. Listen to all of the talk on the radio. Know that you're taking Carlson into custody, but not know about Asher. Explain *that* to me." By the end of her list, she was screaming.

Max put his hand on her shoulder, his face suddenly compassionate. "I truly believe from everything my men have told me, that Asher would want you to know. But I truly can't tell you. His life—in fact, all of the team members' lives—depend on secrecy. You've got to believe we're taking care of him. Kane assured me he will make it."

I'm not going to hit him.

I'm not going to scream.

I might cry.

Leland Hines came back down the stairs from inside the plane. "Eden, you need to get onboard. He really can't tell you anything. Let me help you."

She gave one last pleading look to the big man. "I'm begging you."

"I'm sorry, I can't," Max said gently.

"Come with me, Eden," Leland said as he touched her shoulder. She slowly limped up the stairs and onto the plane.

"God, you have the hardest head in the entire damn world."

Asher winced, but he refused to bend over like his body was aching to do. Really, he shouldn't have yelled.

"You're the stupid ass who climbed up a muddy hill when he just got out of a hospital," Lawson said as he continued to sit on the dilapidated sofa with his boots propped up on the handmade coffee table.

"In my opinion, Ash, that makes you the one with the hardest head."

Asher looked around the cabin. It looked like Lawson had made himself at home. "How long have you been here?"

"Just four days. I was going to go home in two days, but I was into this book." He held up a biography of General George C. Marshall. "It's my final book on generals."

That took Asher a moment to process. Maybe all wasn't lost. *Still...*

Lawson set down his book and grabbed Asher's duffel off of his shoulder. "You really are a stubborn son-of-a-bitch. What the hell were you thinking coming up here? You know I have a satellite phone. You could have gotten ahold of me. Hell, I just saw you two weeks ago, for God's sake. If you wanted to talk to me again, you could have just asked if I was okay, or waited until I was back at Pendleton. What do you want?"

"It's a twofer."

Lawson helped him to the couch. Unfortunately, Asher kind of needed a little bit of help. He felt like shit.

"Okay, let's get number one out of the way, then we can focus on number two. There's tomato soup on the stove."

Asher gave his brother a sideways glance. It was a step up that he wasn't sucking down pea soup. Lawson grinned at him.

"Food first," Asher said. "I'm starving."

On the small little stove, Lawson managed to whip up grilled cheese sandwiches and pour out some tomato soup for both of them.

"If you were like Maman, you would have made a Croque Monsieur," Asher teased.

"You know, if you don't like it, I'll eat your sandwich," Lawson said without heat.

Asher laughed before changing gears and becoming serious. "So, how are you dealing with Xavier's death?"

"Suicide, Ash, suicide."

"I know."

"How?"

Law shot up from the table.

"I fucking hate it. I don't understand it. It makes me mad. I'm so goddamn mad at him!"

He clenched his fists.

Ash looked at his younger brother, whose pain killed him. Worried him.

"And this week?"

"I'm trying to cope. I figured some away-time, other than deep-sea fishing, might help."

"Yep, that was a fucking bust, wasn't it?" Asher laughed. He pushed at Law's chair with his foot, and his brother sat back down.

Lawson rubbed the bridge of his nose. "I don't know. This was all I had. I might be mad, but I miss him, too. I was planning on seeing you next. Been talking to Kane, knew you would be getting out of the hospital tomorrow. Figured I could bunk in your spare room and act as a nurse for a week."

"Just how much leave do you have?"

"A fair amount."

There was that twinkle. Ash was happy to see a Lawson smile. "At least I don't get myself shot so I can get time off. That's a bit extreme, Brother. Shit, you were in the hospital for almost a month."

"Well, speaking of time off, I have a proposition for you. I want to crash a wedding. I would love to have a wingman." Law gave him a double-take.

"Screw that, you just want more time trying to convince me to go to a shrink."

"Like I said in the beginning, it was a twofer."

"Are you planning to object?"

Asher picked up the dishes and put them in the sink. "Nah, I'm after one of the bridesmaids."

"Okay, I'm in. Where is this wedding taking place?"

"Boise."

"When?"

"In four days."

CHAPTER 17

It was like watching a train wreck in slow motion.

"What did you say?" Samantha asked her maid of honor. Eden had no idea how Sam was able to keep her voice calm.

"I love him, and he loves me. Don't tell me you didn't know something was wrong, he's been going out of town every other week for the last six months. Didn't you put it together?"

Eden had been listening to the maid of honor prattle on for over five minutes about the depth of her and the groom's love for one another. She was close to throwing up, and she couldn't stand Sam looking so shellshocked.

"Sheri, it's time for you to leave," Eden said to Sam's cousin.

"No, not until Samantha says she won't marry Kevin."

Eden had had enough. Not hair-pulling enough, but

enough. She grabbed Sheri's arm and pulled. "You're outta here. Go get your man and leave."

"But—" Sam started to say something. "No, you're right, Eden." She turned to the overbearing woman and tilted her head. "Sheri, tell Kevin to leave. Better yet, have him take his groomsmen and his friends and family while he's at it."

"Allow me to take out the trash, Sam."

Sheri jerked her arm out of Eden's grip. "Don't touch me, I'm going."

As she watched the woman's purple-colored ass leave, she considered kicking it, but she somehow managed to stop herself. Instead, Eden slammed the hotel door behind her.

Eden went over to try to hug Samantha, but she held out her hand. "Get me my phone. I need to do something. I need to call Kevin. I need to make sure my cousin isn't lying." Sam bit her lip. Eden could tell she didn't hold out much hope.

Samantha made a facetime call to Kevin.

From the side, Eden saw Kevin's smiling face pop up. Then Sam started talking.

"We've got a problem. Sheri just said you've been having a six-month affair. She's pregnant. I think we need to call off the wedding, don't you?"

Kevin's face turned red, then paled, then crumpled. The weenie had the gall to start crying. *What a fucking wuss.*

"I'm so sorry, Sam. I'm so, so sorry. I can't believe she's pregnant. We were so careful."

Samantha cut off the phone.

Eden moved so she could look at her best friend. She went to hug her, but Sam shook her head. She gulped. "Kevin would have never confessed if I hadn't said the pregnant part. He would have tried to bluff his way through it." Her face turned sour. "I guess that's what happens when you decide to marry your college sweetheart—you know their weak spots."

Eden wanted to go snap the slimy little asshole's neck.

Eden leaned forward to give Sam a hug, but her friend held her off. "I can't, Eden. Once I start crying, I'm never going to stop. I'm supposed to get married in twenty minutes. What do I do? People are already here."

"You let me take care of it," Eden said.

"Eden?"

"Yes, honey?"

"I want my mom."

Eden lightly touched Samantha's shoulder. "I'll get her. She'll be here in just a second, I promise."

Eden headed for the door and prayed that she would see Kevin on the way to finding Sam's mom. The man needed a good kick.

"There's definitely something going on," Asher said as he turned his head to look at the back of the church.

"Yes, it's called a wedding," Lawson replied easily.

"Quit fidgeting. I can't believe you're thirty-one, you're acting like a five-year-old who needs to pee."

"It's supposed to start in five minutes, why isn't the groom in place? Where's the minister?"

"So, they're running a few minutes late. Haven't you ever been to a wedding where that happens?"

"No. We're military, we're on time."

Lawson chuckled. "Settle down, Brother. You look great. Your woman will be here. She'll fall into your arms, you'll have wild monkey sex, all will be good in your world. Okay, maybe not too wild, since she's going to have to do most of the work because of your injury."

An elderly woman who was seated in front of them turned around and winked. Asher bit back a laugh. He really needed to calm down.

He pulled out a hymnal and studied some of the lyrics to a hymn. Then he turned around again to see what was going on.

Nothing.

Now Lawson was laughing.

Asher shut the hymnal. *What the hell is going on? When are things going to start?* He'd been in Boise since last night. He knew where Eden had been staying—Kane had provided that—but A.J. had assured him that she was spending time with the bride and he couldn't intrude. This was killing him.

His head spun at the sound of the back door opening. He didn't care that there should have been activity up at the altar and not the vestibule. He needed to see Eden! Then, as if he had willed it, there she was.

In a vivid two-toned dress that swirled in purple and green. It cut off right at the knees and showed plenty of cleavage. Eden looked gorgeous. She blew him away as she strode up the nave of the church and stopped at the front row on the bride's side. She crouched down to talk to the woman who had to be the mother of the bride. Immediately the woman stood up, and a man stood up beside her. Eden hugged the woman, then stepped out of the way so that they could rush down the aisle.

After they left out the back door, Eden took the two steps right up to the altar, then turned around to face the guests.

"By the look on your face, I'm assuming that's your Eden," Lawson said ruefully. "And if she isn't, I call dibs."

"She's mine, hands off."

"Can I have your attention," Eden called out over the whispering. "I've got some news. The wedding has been called off."

"What happened?" Someone shouted from the back.

"Yeah, what happened?" Someone else asked from the middle.

It was the first moment that Eden looked flustered, but then his lioness stood up straighter and thrust back her shoulders. "You can take back all of your gifts and save them for Kevin and Sheri Alderton's eventual baby shower."

Stunned silence met her words. Then the whispers started.

As straight and tall as a soldier, Eden started her walk

back to the vestibule. Asher got up and slid out so that when she came to his pew he was there. Her eyes widened and her step faltered, but that was her only indication of her surprise. Asher held out his arm. She took it, and they finished the walk out of the church.

He's alive. He's alive. He's alive.

I'm not going to cry.

She could actually feel the heat and strength of him under her fingers. She shot surreptitious glances up to his face. He looked down at her with a heated glance.

Oh, God, this is really happening.

She was going to have a heart attack, right here in the middle of the church. Every single one of her dreams had come true.

Mr. and Mrs. Alderton were practically running to catch up with her and Asher. "Eden, what did you mean about Sheri?"

"They're Sheri's parents. We've got to speed up," Eden hissed at him. Asher easily kept up with her as she ran to the back of the parking lot where she'd parked her rental car.

Wait a minute, he was running pretty good. *He can't be that fucking injured.*

She fumbled with her clutch to get the keys out and unlock the car.

"I'll drive," he said as they got close to the vehicle.

"Just thank your lucky stars that I'm letting you come along," she growled. She jabbed her finger at the passenger door.

There must have been something in her expression that got through to him, because he went to the passenger side and got in.

She pulled out of the parking lot and drove around the block into the Fred Meyer shopping center parking lot. She slammed the car into park and shut off the engine, then turned to Asher and screamed.

"How dare you just show up alive! How dare you not call me!"

He held up his hands. "Eden, let me explain."

She raised a fist to hit him, then held back. "Where can I hit you that won't hurt you?" she demanded to know.

"You're pretty tough. I think anywhere you hit me will hurt."

"Don't try to make me laugh. I'm so damn mad at you, I'm going to scream."

"You've been screaming," he pointed out calmly.

She hit his shoulder. Not hard. If he was any kind of gentleman, he would have flinched.

"Explain," she said as calmly as she could.

Instead, he reached for her, and fool that she was, she fell into his arms. Oh, God, he felt so good. Better than she remembered. Better than all of her dreams. Her hands slid under his suit coat, trying to touch flesh. She wanted to rip the buttons off his shirt.

"Easy," he whispered.

"No."

His fingers were busy undoing her hairdo—bobby pins were falling on the floorboard—and soon he had his fingers tangled in the dark mass. He tilted her head and dove in for a kiss. A kiss that tasted of need, of desperation.

Eden managed not to melt. She needed him too much. She dug her fingers into his shoulders and opened her mouth, sucking his tongue inside, suckling him, doing all she could to keep him close, to prove to herself that he was real, that he was hers and not leaving.

He moved so that his hot hands cupped her cheeks. It took a long moment for her to realize that his thumbs were brushing away teardrops. She broke the kiss and looked up at him through tear-filled eyes. *Dammit, I told myself I wasn't going to cry.*

"Why didn't you call? I don't get it. Why didn't you call?"

"Honey, for the first couple of weeks I wasn't in any shape to call anyone. They ended up calling my brother. Mom flew in from Belgium."

"You could have died?" she wailed. "And I would never have known."

"Kane and Law would have told you. Kane would have known to call."

"But why didn't he? I wanted to be there."

He hugged her close to his chest. "Next time you will be, I promise."

She shoved away from him and he gave an

abbreviated groan. "There better fucking not be a next time, Sailor. And I better damn well be notified next time. What's changed?" She demanded to know as she glared up at him. Her emotions were all over the place, she was happy and mad and so freaking thankful. She wanted to eat him up and hold him close and never let him go.

"You're my woman. The guys know that now."

She arched her brow. "They do? How do they know that?"

"I'm here, aren't I?"

She thought about making it harder on him, but why? He was right where she wanted him to be. And she was in his arms, right where she wanted to be. She pulled his head down for another kiss. He shook his head.

"Hold up. Are you sharing a room with anybody? If you are, we have to check into a new one, because I'm rooming with Lawson."

"You're here with your brother? I want to meet him."

"You can in a couple of days."

Her entire body tingled at his words. "I like your plan, and no, I'm not rooming with anyone. I'm checking out tomorrow though."

His hand cupped her breast. "Not now you aren't."

A loud sound interrupted their reverie.

A teenaged skateboarder had just slammed the flat of his hand on the hood of Eden's rental. "Get a room," he called out.

They looked at one another and laughed.

Asher stared at Eden. He'd never seen a woman look so beautiful before. She was perfect. From the top of her chocolate-brown hair, to her pink swollen lips and witchy green eyes, down to her tiny feet in silver heels.

"You're so keeping this dress," he murmured as he reached behind her and started tugging on the zipper.

"Not so fast," Eden shook her head. "I want to inspect the military's medical job and see if you're up for any physical activity.

"Lady, I'm so up for this you'd be amazed."

Eden snorted. Then she went back to being serious. In her heels she came up to his nose, so she was able to slide his suitcoat off his shoulders. They both let it fall to the carpet floor.

"I like the suspenders," she smiled.

"I didn't have a choice, A belt isn't in the cards for me at the moment."

She frowned as he started to unclip them, and she brushed his fingers aside. He let his arms fall to his sides. He understood her need to do this. Then as she started to unbutton his dress shirt, he watched the expressions flash over her face as she saw the new scars on his body. He really wished she didn't have to see them.

Eden sucked in her breath when she saw the large, still-pink scar. At least it was no longer swollen and inflamed. He'd been lucky—they'd saved both kidneys—even though it had been touch-and-go. He'd lost part of his liver. It was the infection that almost killed him.

She didn't ask any silly questions, she just said, "we're doing this slow and easy."

She's out of her mind.

When she started for the buttons on his slacks, he stilled her fingers. "Now you."

"Okay."

She let him unzip her dress. He had to peel it off her, and when he did, he found just a thong and silver thigh-high stockings.

"Woman, you are an angel. Thank you for this." He traced the skin between the top of her stocking and the gusset of her panties, and she shuddered. She grabbed for his shoulders.

"Asher," she sighed. "Now can you take off your pants?"

"Pretty soon."

He would've liked to have carried her to the bed, but that just wasn't in the cards at the moment. He guided her the five steps backwards, helping her to sink down. As soon as she was seated, he pushed her torso down and stripped off her silk underwear.

He'd dreamed of pleasuring her this way. He'd dreamed of doing everything with this woman. He spread her thighs and put both of her legs over his shoulders.

"You don't have to do this," Eden's voice was hopeful. Asher wasn't sure which way she was hoping, but it didn't matter. He figured that she was going to end up happy.

"I know, but I really want to, is that okay?" he had to ask.

"I guess so."

Good enough for me. Eden's flesh was already glistening with her need. Her scent scattered all thoughts from his brain. He'd already been rock-hard, now he thought his cock would explode just from the look and fragrance of her. God knew what was going to happen when he tasted her, but he was dying to find out.

Asher licked at her delicate folds and she gave a long, loud sigh of pleasure. He parted her flesh so that he could lap up even more of her passion.

"Ashhhhh..."

He lifted the hood of her clit and sucked at the sensitive nub. He felt her moving and looked up to see her sitting up to watch what he was doing, her face suffused with passion. That was his lioness, claiming their loving. Participating every step of the way.

"This feels so good." She sounded surprised.

Ash gently inserted two fingers into the tender entrance of her vagina and started a slow rhythm that had Eden flopping back down onto the bed. Asher grinned, he was onto something. He circled her clit with his tongue and continued to massage her slick channel. Her passion was a miracle. He should have realized that such a fierce fighter would grab hold and match him. He was dying to sink inside her, but first, he needed to pleasure her.

"Cock. Now."

"Ouch." Ash stopped sucking when Eden grabbed his hair. She was staring him in the face.

"I want us to make love now. Please?" she begged.

He laughed.

"What is it, Honey? *Cock now*, or *make love*?"

She bit her lip. "What's going to get you out of your pants the fastest? Tell me and I'll say it."

"Then lean back and let me make you come." He kissed her. All that time, his fingers kept up the torturous pace, but now his thumb was circling her clit. He felt her shivering. She was close. Asher leaned forward and took a swollen nipple into his mouth.

"Ashhh..."

God, she smelled like peaches.

The shivering turned to shuddering. "I'm so close."

He flicked his thumb harder on her sensitive bud, while he enjoyed himself at her breast. She was so soft, even better than his memories. No, he hadn't been wrong, he was all kinds of right about everything.

He felt her melt against his fingers as she shook in orgasm and grabbed his head against her heart. After the long last tremor ended, she looked at him. "Please be with me. Please?"

Asher grabbed a condom out of his pants pocket and then shucked out of them. He moved beside her. Her fingers tangled gently in his chest hair. "I don't want you to hurt," she whispered.

He took her hand and brought it to curl around his erection. "This is what's hurting. Please help put me out of my misery," he laughed roughly.

She stroked him up and down. He handed her the condom and she opened it. Then he slid it on.

She gave him a wary look. "Should I be on top?"

Asher winced at the thought of anything being on top of his incision. "Uhm, no. I think we're going for missionary, Honey. If that works for you." He smiled down at her.

"I've dreamed about being wrapped in your arms, covered by you, having you inside me. That would be perfect."

Asher closed his eyes so he could get himself under control. She still had a way of creating pictures in his mind. Asher couldn't take in enough of Eden's body—she was like a beautiful sultry banquet, created just for him. The stockings had to come off. He needed to see her, not any prop.

As he started to roll down the thigh-high from her right leg, she protested.

"I thought you liked those."

"Not as much as I love your body. I want your body, heart, mind, and soul laid bare."

He saw her bite her lip.

"Asher—"

"I know I'm asking for a lot, but we'll get there. I almost died. Twice. I know what I want. It's you." He kissed his way down her leg until he got to the bottom of her foot, where he laved the slight scar she had on the bottom of her foot. "Does this hurt?"

She shook her head.

When her stockings were gone, he slid up to wrap his arm around her head, holding her, and then dipped down for a long, slow kiss. When she started undulating upwards, he stroked his hand down her ribcage. He played with her nipple until it pebbled, then he plucked and she groaned.

"More. Harder."

He was happy to oblige. He broke off the kiss and scraped his teeth against the burgeoning bud. He thought she might snatch him bald. She spread her legs wide, and he couldn't resist her invitation.

He positioned the head of his penis at her entrance and started a slow slide into her tight wet depths. He never stopped watching her face, checking for any signs of duress. Her muscles were clamping down on him so hard, he was afraid he was hurting her.

She dug one foot into his ass, avoiding his wounded side.

"Don't hold back or I'll have to hit you again," she gritted out.

Asher barked out a laugh. She lifted her hips and took more of him, then moaned.

"Eden, was that a good sound, or bad sound?"

"So good, let's do it some more." She pressed up again, only this time he pushed downwards. He thought his head would explode as she welcomed all of him. He pinched her nipple, and she groaned.

He had to move. He had to. So, he did. Her smile was ecstatic. She reached out and stroked his jaw. "Oh, Asher, it was just like I dreamed."

He pumped harder and she met him thrust for thrust. He was dying and she was talking. He had to do something to make her come. He moved his hand from her breast and reached between them to touch her clit. She sighed with delight, her eyes closing.

"Open your eyes."

Her lids opened slowly.

He kissed her again. She was his Eden. Her hand moved on the side of his body that wasn't injured. Then her nails dug in as she started to thrash underneath him. She was panting. *So close. Just one more thrust.* She let out a loud moan as her channel clenched his cock so hard, they were fused into one being.

He shuddered and groaned as he released everything into Eden. His heart, his soul. Everything he was.

CHAPTER 18

She snuggled under the hotel duvet but didn't bother with the pillow when she had Asher's chest instead. He'd just gotten done telling her about his time at the hospital. It scared the hell out of her.

"Why do you think they'll let me in next time?"

"I'll put you on the list of people to notify and visit. It'll be fine."

Eden thought about having to drop everything and flying to find out about Asher's health.

"We've been living in a vault again. Only this time there's room service and we could go outside if we wanted to."

He looked down at her. "How do you figure?"

"It's a time out of place. For three days, we've gorged on sex and gotten to know one another. You surprised me when you said your favorite color is yellow. Never would have guessed that, Sailor."

Asher chuckled.

"But we haven't talked once about the future."

He sat up in the bed and put a mound of pillows behind him, hitching her up with him so he could look at her. "No, I've been very clear about the future. You haven't been listening."

"Huh?" That was totally out of left field. He looked serious as a heart attack.

"Asher, I don't know what in the hell you're talking about. You have not once talked about the future."

"Sure, I have. I've made it clear that I want your heart and soul, and you already have mine. What could be more clear than that?"

Oh my God, how did I miss that?
Take a breath. Don't scream.

"Okay, can you be more specific as to what that would look like, say, in the next six months?" she asked slowly.

"Well, I have to live in Virginia for my job. You take translator gigs all over the place, so where you're based doesn't matter. I figured you could stay with me for a bit, then we could find a place that would suit you."

"Asher Thorne, are you asking me to move in with you?"

"I'm not asking, I thought that's what we were doing here. Did I get this wrong?"

Eden laughed.

Asher scowled.

She was now adept at hugging him in such a way she knew wouldn't hurt his injury, so she threw her arms around him. "You have my mind, soul, and heart. I love you, Asher Thorne. I definitely want to live with you."

His smile could light up all of Boise. Hell, it could light up the entire state of Idaho.

"So, does that mean you're up with my plan?"

"It's going to take a little more than a minute to get it accomplished, but absolutely."

She reached up and kissed him with trembling lips.

"I love you too, Eden. More than you can ever know. Heart, mind, and soul."

EPILOGUE

Asher laughed at Eden's nervousness. It was a new look for her. "You know they won't care if the food doesn't come out right on time. As long as the beer is cold, they're good."

The doorbell rang.

"Oh no, somebody's on time."

"Well, sure," Asher smiled.

"Oh, God." Eden disappeared into the kitchen.

"Is she always like this?" he asked her friend, Samantha Brooks. Sam was staying with them for the weekend and had agreed to man the tables in the backyard.

"I've never seen her like this. It's a totally new phenomenon. What have you done to her in the last four months, Ash?"

"Nothing, I swear."

Sam took a sip of her beer. "Now, that's certainly not true, I've gotten some details." She smirked.

Asher felt his face heat. *How come my teammates can give me shit all day long, but the idea of one of Eden's friends knowing something about our sex life scares the hell out of me?*

"I'm going to go see if I can help the hostess, but everything is perfect in the kitchen. I'll see if there's a paper bag for her to breathe into."

That caught Asher up short. "Do you think it's that bad?"

The doorbell rang again.

"Go answer the door. Eden will be fine."

When Asher got to the door, he was confronted with a big bowl of potato salad, courtesy of A.J. McNamara. "I figured that Eden could use some reinforcements. I also brought tequila for her and me. Maybe Carys too, if she isn't on-call."

Standing behind her, Kane shrugged.

"Actually, I think a shot would be welcome at this point. For some reason, she's freaking out." Asher explained.

"Of course, she is. This is the first party she's hosted with your team, and it's in your new house. She wants it to be perfect." She tilted her head. "Is the kitchen that way?"

Asher nodded.

A.J. left to provide aid and comfort in the form of tequila.

"I need a beer," Asher said to Kane.

Kane laughed as he slapped him on the back. "Nice place you have here. I assume it's all Eden's doing?"

"Except for the garage. That's where the beer is."

"I didn't see one when I pulled up into your driveway."

"That's because it's detached and out back. It's pretty slick." Asher made sure to go outside using the kitchen's sliding glass door so he could check on Eden. What he saw made him smile. She and Sam were both laughing at something A.J. was saying. Eden was looking a lot less stressed. Asher relaxed.

"When are you going to ask her to marry you?" Kane asked as they made their way to the garage.

She's going to Europe next week to meet with the prosecutors on Becker's case. I'm flying out to Montana to talk to her dad. Trust me, there is no way I can ask her until I've asked his permission."

"For real?" Kane asked as they got to the garage.

"I'm just happy I don't have to ask all her brothers, too."

Asher opened a cooler and pulled out two beers. He looked up and saw Raiden, Nic, and Ezio coming their way. He pulled out three more.

Eden leaned into Asher as they sat on the picnic bench together. "You did good," he whispered into her hair.

She looked around at all of the empty bowls and platters. Since everybody had a plastic container of food to take home if they wanted it, she felt like it was a success. Now people were all settled and spending time talking. *Yep, the party was a success.* She'd wanted that for Asher.

"When do we get to kick them out?" Asher asked.

She looked up into his blue eyes and laughed. "They'll probably leave by midnight."

He groaned. "That long?"

"Sam's staying here anyway."

"Her bedroom is upstairs. Everything's good." He stroked her lower back. She loved how he could get her hot and bothered by just a touch.

"It's a shame Lawson couldn't make it," Eden said.

"Yeah, he was looking forward to it. But missions come up."

"Do you think he'll finally get some help?" After hearing Asher's last phone call with his brother, she was really hopeful.

"I think so. But I'll have to see it to believe it."

Eden put her arms around Asher, trying to give him comfort.

"It's okay, Honey. I'm not giving up."

"No, you never do," she smiled up at him. "You're it for me, Asher Thorne. I love you."

He looked around their backyard. Everybody was happy, full, and occupied. Asher stood up, drawing Eden up with him.

As he pulled her inside, she laughed. "We can't."

"Oh, we absolutely can."

He walked her down the hall, tugged her into their bedroom, locked the door, and pulled Eden into his arms.

"Eden, your trust in me is a gift. Thank you for that. I love you; body, heart, mind, and soul."

He was her gift. He was the man she would always choose to protect her.

"Did you see that?" Samantha Brooks laughed up at Ezio Stark. "I think we've been abandoned by our hosts."

Ezio looked down at the beautiful blonde who he'd been talking to half the night. "I did see that. I think that means we could make our getaway. What do you say?"

THE END

Read Ezio and Samantha's Story in *Her Intense Protector*, Night Storm Book 4

Read Lawson and Jill's Story in *Lawson & Jill*, Night Storm Legacy Novel 1

Many lives are touched by the tragedy of suicide. If you or a loved one is thinking of

suicide or dealing with issues related to suicide, please call the National Suicide Prevention Lifeline at 1-800-273-TALK (8255) or the Suicide Crisis Line at 1-800-784-2433.

ABOUT THE AUTHOR

USA Today Bestselling Author, Caitlyn O'Leary, adores writing Military Romantic Suspense and Paranormal Romance. She started publishing books in 2014. Storytelling has been a tradition in her family for years, and she still holds on to the letters she has received from family members since her childhood.

Caitlyn lives in California with her husband John of sixteen years who often makes guest appearances in her reader group, Caitlyn's Crew. Getting to know so many people within the reader community is almost as much fun as writing each new novel. So join her reader group so she can get to know you, and see if she and John can make it to year seventeen!

You never know what kind of book she'll write next, it all depends on what strikes her fancy. Be sure to keep in touch.

Keep up with Caitlyn O'Leary:

Website: www.caitlynoleary.com
Email: caitlyn@caitlynoleary.com

Newsletter: http://bit.ly/1WIhRup

- facebook.com/Caitlyn-OLeary-Author-638771522866740
- twitter.com/CaitlynOLearyNA
- instagram.com/caitlynoleary_author
- amazon.com/author/caitlynoleary
- bookbub.com/authors/caitlyn-o-leary
- goodreads.com/CaitlynOLeary
- pinterest.com/caitlynoleary35

ALSO BY CAITLYN O'LEARY

Night Storm Series

Her Ruthless Protector (Book #1)

Her Tempting Protector (Book #2)

Her Chosen Protector (Book #3)

Her Intense Protector (Book #4)

Night Storm Legacy Series

Lawson & Jill (Book 1)

The Midnight Delta Series

Her Vigilant Seal (Book #1)

Her Loyal Seal (Book #2)

Her Adoring Seal (Book #3)

Sealed with a Kiss (Book #4)

Her Daring Seal (Book #5)

Her Fierce Seal (Book #6)

A Seals Vigilant Heart (Book #7)

Her Dominant Seal (Book #8)

Her Relentless Seal (Book #9)

Her Treasured Seal (Book #10)

Black Dawn Series

Her Steadfast Hero (Book #1)
Her Devoted Hero (Book #2)
Her Passionate Hero (Book #3)
Her Wicked Hero (Book #4)
Her Guarded Hero (Book #5)
Her Captivated Hero (Book #6)
Her Honorable Hero (Book #7)
Her Loving Hero (Book #8)

THE FOUND SERIES

Revealed (Book #1)
Forsaken (Book #2)
Healed (Book #3)

SHADOWS ALLIANCE SERIES

Declan

Made in the USA
Middletown, DE
16 November 2022